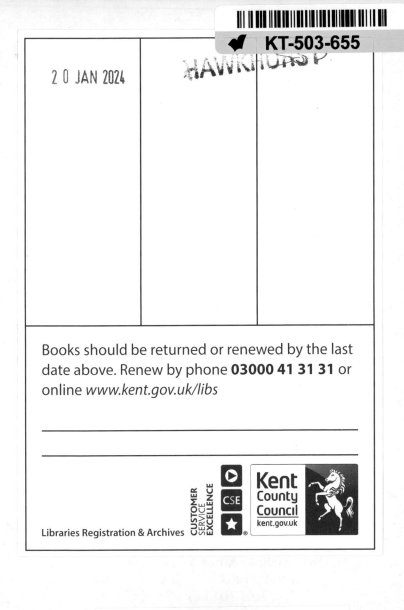

A HERO'S WELCOME

Wounded during the American War of Independence, all Robert Lester wants is to return home to Nottinghamshire. But when he arrives, feverish and drenched by a storm, he finds his mother and sister missing and an attractive stranger living in their cottage. Ellen Fairfax, a young widow with a small son, offers him shelter for the night. But Ellen is hiding from her past, and her act of kindness puts all that is most precious to her in jeopardy . . .

JASMINA SVENNE

◆

A HERO'S
WELCOME

Complete and Unabridged

LINFORD
Leicester

First published in Great Britain in 2015

First Linford Edition
published 2016

A catalogue record for this book is available
from the British Library.

ISBN 978–1–4448–2769–9

Published by
F. A. Thorpe (Publishing)
Anstey, Leicestershire

Set by Words & Graphics Ltd.
Anstey, Leicestershire
Printed and bound in Great Britain by
T. J. International Ltd., Padstow, Cornwall

This book is printed on acid-free paper

1

'Do you need any help, sir?'

'No, no, I can manage,' Robert Lester replied irritably, and then wondered a second later if he had been overhasty. The ostler had meant well and he should not have been so quick to take offence.

The trouble was, he thought as he struggled to negotiate the steps of the stagecoach, that for much of the time he simply forgot about his wooden leg and crutches. At night sometimes he even felt twinges of pain or an annoying itch in the toes of his missing foot. But the amputation was still too recent for him to have acquired all the instinctive knowledge he needed about how to move in every situation.

He swayed dangerously as he tottered to the ground. A large, strong hand shot out and gripped his elbow to steady him, but the ostler said nothing.

'Thank you,' Robert mumbled, ashamed of his earlier gruffness.

The man merely grinned and gave him the awkward salute of a civilian in deference to the red coat Robert still wore, though his commission had been sold to the most senior ensign in his former regiment.

'Will you be wanting a room for the night, sir?'

Robert turned towards the speaker. The broad-shouldered man — evidently the landlord of the Swan — was a stranger. It unnerved Robert, reminding him of how long he had been away from Nottinghamshire.

'That won't be necessary. But perhaps you could find a safe place to stow my luggage until I can send someone to fetch it?'

'Certainly, sir.'

In olden days he would have been able to carry his own knapsack. But for now Robert wanted to get home as quickly as possible, unhindered by anyone or anything. Now he was so close, all his anxieties about his family felt more urgent than ever.

Thrusting enough money in the landlord's hand to ensure none of his meagre possessions went astray, Robert set off at a steady pace, swinging along on his crutches as rapidly and smoothly as he was able after being crammed into a stagecoach for four days. The sooner he reached less populated areas, the safer he would feel.

He did not particularly want to be recognised in Mansfield, though he knew it was a possibility. He had grown up in the vicinity of the market town, his father having been the steward of Mr Longridge, an elderly gentleman whose house, the Grange, was situated a mile beyond the town.

Robert felt he would prefer it if his family were the first to hear of his return. Besides, he knew what a fuss his parents' friends would make, in the kindest possible way, about his lost leg, and he did not feel he could cope with that just yet.

A great many things had changed since he had last been here. Shop signs had faded or been repainted, or had simply been altered when businesses changed hands. A ramshackle, half-timbered cottage had been pulled down and a smart sandstone townhouse was being erected in its place. The old yew in the churchyard had lost one of its stoutest branches. The whole thing seemed unreal. That child toddling after its mother towards the pump had probably not even been born when Robert had set out for America in 1775.

While he had been away, he had taken comfort in the idea that this place was unchanging — something he could come back to once the American rebels had backed down and agreed to abide by the existing laws and everything could return to normality.

Not that he had spent much time in Mansfield in recent years. Even before his regiment had been sent abroad, they had been garrisoned in various towns the length and breadth of the country.

Oh, he had tried to visit his parents and his younger sister whenever he had leave. But those occasions were rare and his last visit had been particularly painful. Not only had he come to say farewell before embarking for America, but he had also had to attend his father's funeral.

Now his career was over. He would never be a colonel, with or without his own regiment. He would never even have risen above the rank of sergeant in peacetime, and certainly not as high as lieutenant, or not in such a relatively short period. But the war still stuttered on, much longer than anyone had anticipated, as perhaps all wars do.

No, Robert told himself, he would not think about the war now. He would only think of happy things; about the smiles and tears of joy with which Mamma and Polly would greet him.

But even there his worries drew him up short.

It was not that he feared they would love him less for his missing leg. It was a sign, after all, that he had done his duty; had been at the forefront of his men to encourage them on; had not shirked in the face of danger. Of course he knew his family would be upset on his behalf. But even that was not the worst of it.

Why had he not received a single letter from home since being wounded? Could his letter home telling them about it have miscarried? If that were so, neither his mother nor Polly would be prepared for his injury. And how on earth would he be able to earn his keep and support them now?

'Come back in one piece,' Polly had urged him on that last day, as she picked a stray hair off his red coat so she wouldn't have to meet his eyes.

'I will, I promise.'

Robert twitched, physically trying to avoid the memory, and threw himself off balance. He rested a moment on his crutches, aware suddenly of how tired his arms were from his exertions. He had not paced himself well. He had overestimated his strength in his eagerness to get beyond the outskirts of the town. There was still at least half a mile to go, past meadows and woodland, and uphill all the way.

Moreover, it was possible he still had a touch of the fever he had caught in the American wilderness. He had done his best to pretend he was only suffering from the effects of the coach journey, but at times he felt light-headed and shaky.

There was no longer any hurry, however. He had been afraid his faded scarlet coat might attract attention in the town, but this was a little-used lane, leading nowhere apart from to the Grange and, beyond it, the village of Blidworth.

There had been little opportunity for Robert to acquire civilian dress. At first there had been the pain and the shock of the amputation to recover from. Then the journey home, for what had felt like months, on a ship crammed with other wounded soldiers and widows with fatherless children, returning to who knew what in England.

It had been a rough crossing from New York because it was still so early in the season. Robert had had few chances to practise tottering around on his crutches on shipboard, and much of the strength he had acquired while convalescing in New York had been lost in the six or seven weeks on the Atlantic Ocean.

By the time he reached Portsmouth, he had had enough of the sea and had elected to continue his journey in a series of coaches, instead of sailing as far as London. The nearer he grew to his destination, the more impatient he had become. Yes, there had been much to distress him in the past months. Yes, it would upset his family to see his wooden leg. But he was, despite the odds, still alive. He was sure that if he could reach the bosom of his family, he would grow strong again within a matter of months and would be able to contemplate what he should do with the rest of his life.

A chill breeze insinuated itself through Robert's coat. He shivered as he looked up. He had not noticed those blue-black clouds gathering on the horizon. The sun was only a white-gold eye amid the darkening mass. If he didn't hurry, night and the storm would overtake him.

With renewed vigour, he swung his crutches forward and eased his body after them. Prod and swing, prod and swing. He placed one of the crutches accidentally on a loose pebble, which rolled out from under it. He managed to remain upright, but the effort left him shaken and breathless. While he was nerving himself to go on, the first icy raindrop splattered against his cheek.

There was not a moment to be lost. Soon, very soon, he would be able to see the house, beyond the thicket. Wasn't that perhaps the gleam of a window between the nodding branches and sparse leaves? Couldn't that be a wisp of smoke from the chimney, mingling with the clouds?

Raindrops beat like hooves on the crown of his tricorn hat. The sandy path was turning dark where the rain had soaked in. A drop stung his hand. Another exploded behind his collar, like a snowball hurled by a mischievous child.

Never had the urge to run pulsed more wildly through Robert's veins. *Just a little further, just a little further*, pattered the rain on the new leaves of the trees.

And there it was, just as he remembered it: the neat cottage of honey-coloured sandstone, the parlour window glowing like an ember.

He guessed his mother and sister might be thinking of him, even if they did not utter his name out loud. Perhaps they had already received his last letter, sent from Portsmouth to inform them that he had landed on British soil. They were probably sitting, each on her own side of the hearth, sewing shirts for his homecoming or reading the newspaper, following each rumour and misrepresentation about the war, or poring over a map of the American Colonies to try to find Brandywine Creek or Germantown or Saratoga, or any of the other places they had never heard of before.

And then doubts assailed him again. It seemed such a long time since he had heard from them. Suppose something was wrong. Suppose someone was ill, or . . .

No. He put that thought from his mind. That unwavering light in the window could not deceive him. Mamma would have let him know if anything was amiss.

He struggled to negotiate round the gate, but he refused to leave it open for fear of letting out the dog, if they had acquired a new one to replace their father's old pointer. He limped up the path between the still-barren vegetable beds. Propping himself as best he could on one crutch, he raised his hand to the latch. Then he stopped himself. He would not alarm them by barging in on them unannounced. Instead he rapped at the door.

As he waited, half-sheltered by the eaves from the worst of the storm, he became aware that he was soaked to the skin. In the dim light his hands looked raw from the stinging rain, and droplets dripped from the cocked brim of his hat. He closed his eyes for a second. The old, familiar fever pains swirled through his body.

Footsteps pattered inside. The door was opened a crack and one eye appeared.

'Who's there?' a voice demanded.

'Jane? Is that you? It's me, Lieutenant Lester. Can I come in?'

He pushed the door a little wider to reveal a short, plump woman, past the first flush of youth, in the simple garb of a servant. It was not his mother's maid, or anyone else he remembered.

The sight of yet another stranger checked him. The maid, too, would not let go of the door and barred the opening with her own body.

'I beg your pardon,' Robert began, but the maid interrupted him.

'Who are you? What do you want?'

She took in first his shabby coat, then his crutches and wooden leg. At least, Robert assumed that was what caused the sharp intake of her breath.

'You must be new,' he said, forcing his stiff cheek muscles into what he hoped was a reassuring smile. 'I'm Robert Lester, Mrs Lester's son. I've come home.'

Still the woman would not budge; and when he tried to step forward, she swung the door towards him so it struck his shoulder.

'You must've mistaken the house. There's no one here of that name.'

Fear had begun to spread through Robert's body, but he refused to give

13

way to it. There must be a mistake. He had not made himself clear or had uttered his name too indistinctly. And it was not surprising that a maid in a household of women would be wary of letting in a stranger, even one with only one leg. Perhaps she thought he was a beggar or an impostor.

'My father used to be Mr Longridge's steward. He said my mother and sister could stay on here even after my father's death.'

Why on earth was the maid looking at him in that strange way?

'I'm sorry, sir, but — '

'Damn it all, if you would only ask your mistress to come and speak to me for a moment, I'm sure all this could be resolved in no time.'

Robert could feel his patience snapping as the chill sank deeper into his aching bones. His head was throbbing, making it hard for him to formulate logical sentences. The maid hesitated and glanced over her shoulder towards the parlour door. At that moment,

Robert heard the voice of a young woman, calling from within the room.

'Polly? Polly, is that you?' All his impatience surged to his head. Finding strength and agility he had not thought he still possessed, he thrust open the door and tottered past the maid before she could react. 'It's me, Robert. I've come home . . .'

The parlour door sprang open and a young woman in a black gown appeared. Robert blinked in the light that streamed from the parlour. Everything swam. He could not seem to focus his eyes. Suddenly he felt very ill and cold, his limbs shaking from recent exertion, his muscles aching and pulsing.

The maid was squawking some protest, but Robert did not even hear her. Instead he kept staring at the woman in black.

'What is it, sir? Can I help you?' she asked, smiling as she took a step forward.

A woman with dark, glossy hair and

15

grey-blue eyes in an oval face. A woman who, no matter how long he stared at her, was not his sister, though she was about Polly's age.

'My sister, my mother,' he stammered. Who was this woman? Why was she here? 'Where are they? I've come home. I — '

He was forced to lean against the wall so he could press the heel of his hand to his throbbing forehead. Those dove-grey eyes were still on his face. They seemed to have a paralysing effect on his mind and his tongue. He saw her expression change from polite enquiry to bewilderment to — yes, compassion.

'You're ill, sir,' she said gently, coming closer and extending her hand. 'Why don't you come into the parlour and sit down, and as soon as the rain is past I'll send Maggie to fetch the physician.'

'No, no, no!' He had reached the end of his tether. 'I've had enough of doctors. All I want to know is where my family is and what you are doing in their house.'

Her expression changed again. He had flinched from her touch and her hand dropped by her side.

'Come into the parlour, sir,' she said. 'I'll explain there.'

'No, you can explain here. Who are you? What are you doing here?'

The maid twitched, as if asking her mistress for permission to intervene or run for help. But the lady gestured at her to close the outer door instead.

'I'm very sorry, sir,' she said. 'My name is Ellen Fairfax. I am Mr Longridge's new tenant.'

Robert uttered a croak deep inside his throat. He could feel the nightmare beginning to envelop him.

'Where are they?' he whispered. Surely, surely they could not be dead. Not both of them. And yet, there had been no replies to his letters . . .

Ellen Fairfax hesitated before she answered, still keeping her eyes on his. 'I'm sorry. I have really no idea. I've only been here a month, but I gather the house had stood empty for some time prior to that.'

The black cloud Robert had felt menacing him ever since he had first set foot in the house now blotted out the last of the light. He heard a woman cry out and was aware for a second of a slim but strong arm wrapping about his waist — and then he plunged into deeper darkness.

2

Consciousness returned slowly to Robert. He was aware that he was lying on his side. He could hear a fire crackling; feel its heat on his face. Everything ached. He felt sick and could not have moved to save his life.

Other things came to him by degrees. His boot had been removed. Hands were prying at his stock, pulling it free so it slithered round the back of his neck. A woman's voice crooned like a distant dove.

'Thank you, Maggie,' another voice answered close by, and he felt a blanket spread over him and tickle his chin.

The coolness of a damp cloth on his forehead made him jolt. The sharp tang of eau de cologne struck his nostrils and stung the back of his throat. He shivered. But the coolness was soothing as well. Rain, perhaps hail, was beating at the window, and from somewhere far, far away he thought he heard the wail of a small child.

'Go and see to him, Maggie,' the woman closest to him said. He heard a rustle of silk, as if she had turned or risen. 'I can manage here.'

The door closed reluctantly and the voice of the child was cut off. For an instant Robert felt a shadow hovering above him. Then it moved away. He heard soft noises travel around the room, interrupted by a dull thud and a stifled mutter of annoyance.

Robert opened his eyes cautiously, wary of the light. He didn't think he had moved sufficiently to attract attention, but he heard a sudden rustle. A woman's face appeared above him, then sank down beside him.

'Feeling any better?' she asked.

He did not have the strength to reply.

'I thought, if you were strong enough, we might be able to get you upstairs to one of the bedrooms,' the woman — Ellen Something — went on.

20

Her lips fluttered and he realised that she was trying to conceal her unease. 'Maggie has made up the bed, but I'm afraid you'll have to climb the stairs yourself, because even together, we're not strong enough to carry you. It took all our efforts to get you this far.'

She was talking too much because she seemed afraid of silence, or perhaps of the questions he might ask. Looking around, he felt another wave of disorientation. The couch on which he lay, the armchair against which his crutches had been propped, the very hearthrug on which his boot stood steaming — all the trappings of his old life were here, in this house. Only its inhabitants had changed.

'You'll be able to manage it, won't you, if I assist you?' Ellen went on, the anxious look still in her eyes. 'Or if you cannot face it, I suppose we could nurse you here; only I thought you'd be more comfortable in a proper bed, where you could stretch out and there would be no danger that you might fall and hurt yourself.'

'No, I won't impose on you,' Robert said with an effort. 'I must go — '

Where? Back to the coaching inn?

'Nonsense. I won't hear of it. I wouldn't turn a rabid dog out on a night like this, much less . . . In any case, you're in no fit state to go anywhere, and I'm afraid I'm not wealthy enough to keep horses or a carriage, so I would be forced to send Maggie out to hire or borrow a conveyance.'

While she was speaking, Robert had managed to haul himself up on one elbow and from there to a seated position, but the blood rushed to his head.

'There you go, that's the way,' his hostess said a touch too heartily as she removed the compress from his forehead.

She picked up the blanket he had pushed aside and whipped it around his shoulders like a cloak. He was, he realised, shivering convulsively, and nothing seemed to be left of his former strength.

She passed him one of his crutches, and with its aid he hauled himself up, but a fresh wave of giddiness assailed him. Again a slim arm entwined his waist.

'If you lean on me, sir, I think we'll be able to manage,' she said.

Her shoulders were just the right height for him to lean on. The thought crossed his mind and then he felt a twinge of shame at burdening a woman like this.

'If you'll pass me my other crutch, I'll — '

Damn. His boot. He could feel the smoothness of the floorboards through his stocking. He had got up too soon. He should have donned his boot first, ready to face the world outside.

'I really think this might be better,' Ellen objected. 'A crutch couldn't save you if you had another dizzy spell. You are dizzy, aren't you?'

He couldn't deny it. He let her guide

him towards the hall, but there again he resisted her attempts to lure him up the stairs.

'Really, Miss — I've forgotten your name.'

'Mrs Fairfax.' She uttered the name softly but firmly and suddenly her black gown and plain cap made sense to him.

'Oh. Well then, Mrs Fairfax, I cannot stay here, not anymore. If you'll let me rest a little while longer, I'm sure I am capable of making my own way back to town.'

'I won't hear of it — not in this weather, not in your state of health. I can feel how feverish you are. Now, we can stand here and argue all night, and I can keep your other crutch hostage, and you can try to wear me down with your weight; but I am not going to budge on this matter.'

'I'm not your responsibility. Why should you take so much trouble over me?'

'You're a soldier,' she replied firmly.

Then her voice shook. 'So was my husband.'

Her directness undid his last defences. He allowed her to take away his remaining crutch so he could grasp the banister with one hand, while tightening his grip around her shoulders with the other arm.

It took all his willpower to concentrate. How many times had he run up and down these stairs, to say nothing of sliding down the banister? He took as much of his weight as he could on the arm that was clutching the banister, so he would not crush Ellen Fairfax under his weight. If he lost his balance, he might send them both crashing down into the hall.

He was so exhausted by the time he reached the top of the stairs that he meekly allowed Ellen Fairfax to lead him through the nearest door, to what had once been his bedroom, and guide him to the bed. He closed his eyes as he lay down, willing the world to stop whirling. And then he realised his coat had already been unbuttoned and his self-appointed nurse was attempting to ease one of his arms out of its sleeve.

'No,' he protested, but somehow gave way to her as she rolled him from side to side so she could remove first his coat, then his waistcoat.

Her touch was light, cool and soothing. A fresh compress was placed carefully upon his forehead. Then, while his attention was distracted, he realised she had undone the buckles at the knees of his breeches and unfastened his garter so she could peel off his rain-sodden stocking.

Robert sank deeper into the pillows, almost resigned. She had gone so far already. What difference would it make if she removed the wooden leg too and left him only with the stump?

He jerked half-upright again at her next action. The compress fell from his forehead onto his chest, soaking his shirt. But ignoring his protest and his attempts to prise her fingers away, she had already unbuttoned his flies.

'I am — or was — a married woman,' she said, but her cheeks were scarlet and she could not meet his eyes.

She pressed him back down on the pillow and replaced the compress. Fortunately his shirt was long enough to preserve his modesty and as quickly as possible, Ellen Fairfax tucked the covers around him. Then she hovered for a moment.

'I forgot to ask — are you hungry? I'm sure Maggie could fetch something from the kitchen.'

But he shook his head, much too sick to contemplate food. 'No, thank you. It's very kind of you, but . . . ' He trailed away into an awkward silence.

'Well, I'd better leave you. Try to sleep it off,' she said, laying her hand briefly against his cheek before she turned away from the bed and vanished, leaving behind only the scent of spring flowers.

⋆　⋆　⋆

'How are you this morning?'

Ellen forced herself to smile as she approached the bedside of her reluctant patient. It had taken all her nerve to tap at his door. She didn't want to betray how self-conscious she felt, having had a whole night to recall how she had manhandled this handsome stranger into bed.

There were also wider implications to what she had done. People were so apt to misinterpret the most innocent actions. And yet what choice had she had? She couldn't have turned him outdoors, when he was so ill and the weather so appalling.

But not for the first time, she suppressed the suggestion that insinuated its way into her mind that she could and should have sent Maggie to the Grange to ask her cousin Philip for help.

'I'm much better,' Robert Lester croaked.

'Then there's no need to send for a doctor?'

'None whatsoever.'

'Good. I'm glad,' Ellen replied. 'Maggie is making breakfast and thought you might like some toast?'

'Toast — yes, that would be . . . most acceptable,' Mr Lester replied, but he had dropped his head so he would not have to meet her eye.

'Is there anything else you need?' Ellen asked, sensing something unspoken.

Slowly, he ran his fingers along his jaw. 'Well, I would quite like to shave,' he admitted with a rueful smile, 'but I'm afraid I left all my belongings at the Swan Inn.'

Ellen felt the laceration of a fleeting memory. But she knew she was being foolish. There was, of course, only one thing she could do.

'Leave it to me,' she said. 'I think I can help.'

And, not wanting to answer the question that inevitably sprang to his lips, she hastened to her bedroom next door.

After a lifetime of being billeted here, there and everywhere, moving from one garrison town to the next, she was still not used to having a room of her own. It still felt like a miracle that she could go to the dressing table and know that if she opened a certain drawer, it would contain all the things she had kept that had belonged to James, which, in time, she would pass on to her son.

There they all were, her little treasures. James's gold watch, salvaged by one of his fellow officers. The portrait he had given her before he had set sail for America, alone, because she had been far too heavily pregnant to travel with him. Every letter he had ever written to her, tied up with a faded red ribbon that had once adorned her best gown, the one she had worn on the night when James had first danced with her.

But she could not dwell on such things, not now. Instead her hand stretched out to pick up the small leather case that contained James's shaving kit, the very same one he had taken with him everywhere when he was on campaign. She had kept it because it evoked so many memories of their last days together in New York. But she couldn't afford to be sentimental about something so prosaic. Blinking away tears and plastering a smile on her lips, she returned to the sickroom.

'Here we are,' she said, holding out the battered leather pouch.

Robert Lester looked down as he took the case, then glanced at her face. He didn't ask where it had come from. Ellen could tell from the look in his eyes that he had guessed and suddenly she knew that if he were too sympathetic, she would not be able to prevent herself from crying.

She whisked away to fetch a hand mirror and some warm water from the washstand. 'I think perhaps you'd better not get up just yet, don't you?' she said. In spite of her attempts to sound cheerful, she could hear the wobble in her voice. 'You'll be able to shave sitting down, won't you, if I hold the mirror for you?'

She was afraid of allowing the room to grow silent; afraid that her grief might get the better of her, despite the fact that more than a year had passed since James's death. She had thought she was much more in control of her emotions than this.

'Of course I can manage,' Robert Lester replied, and Ellen felt a shudder pass down her spine because she had almost expected to hear James's voice.

He helped her clear a space on the bedside table for the bowl of water, a mug, a stick of soap, a towel, the razor and the shaving brush. Ellen couldn't help noticing that his hand shook as he lathered his face. He was forced to close his eyes while he nerved himself to pick up the razor, as if waiting for a spell of dizziness to pass.

Ellen made a decision. While his eyes were still closed, she set aside the mirror and picked up the cut-throat razor. Carefully she unfolded it and tested its edge. Contrary to her expectations, it still seemed sharp enough not to need stropping.

'What are you doing with that?'

Robert Lester's eyes had popped open and there was no disguising the alarm in his voice.

'Hold very still,' Ellen replied, hoping her own hand would remain steady. 'You don't think this is the first time I've done this, do you?'

But there was a world of difference between shaving your own husband when he was unwell and shaving a complete stranger, Ellen thought ruefully. The fear of causing a serious cut was just the same, but she could not banter with Robert Lester, as she would have done with James.

She felt herself flushing, conscious of his intent gaze upon her face, even though she dared not look up. Instead she kept her eyes fixed upon his jaw and mouth — trying not to notice the endearing dimple in his chin, or the sensuous fullness of his lower lip.

Neither of them spoke until she was done. Contrary to her fears, however, she managed to complete the delicate task without causing a single nick.

'There.' Ellen couldn't hide the relief or the triumph in her voice as she wiped the blade clean for the last time. 'What do you think?'

She offered him the hand mirror. She was gratified by the smile Robert Lester gave her as he ran one hand along his jaw and twisted his head from side to side while admiring himself in the mirror.

'Evidently you have missed your calling,' he said. 'I feel I owe you an apology for doubting you, Mrs Fairfax, as well as my heartfelt thanks.'

'Think nothing of it.'

The warmth of his gaze made her blush again and she turned aside to clear away the shaving gear.

'Mrs Fairfax?'

'Yes?'

'May I ask you something?'

'That depends on what it is.' But Ellen smiled to demonstrate he was not meant to take her words too literally.

'It's just that — I've been wondering how you came to be living here in the steward's house?' She hesitated and he added hastily, 'I mean, you are not from this part of Nottinghamshire, are you? I'm sure I would remember you if you were, and I don't suppose Mr Longridge employs you as his steward, so I wondered . . . ' His voice trailed away, as if he feared he was venturing into delicate territory.

'Oh, it's simple enough.' Ellen decided to tackle the most straightforward part of his enquiry first. 'Philip Longridge is my cousin. I don't know if you know that he inherited the Grange a few months ago when his uncle died? Anyway, this house chanced to fall vacant at around the same time that I happened to need new lodgings, so he suggested I should come and live here. That's all.'

It was not, in fact, quite all, but Ellen

did not see that there was any need to tell this new acquaintance why she had found her previous lodgings insupportable. However, having been in the army himself, Robert Lester clearly had no difficulty in accepting that an officer's widow might find herself adrift and dependent on the kindness of relatives. He nodded slowly.

'Yes, I assumed it must be something like that,' he said, but she could tell from the frown gathering on his forehead that he had turned his mind back to the more personal question of the whereabouts of his family.

'I'm sure . . . ' she began, but the sudden sound of tottering footsteps on the stairs cut her short. 'Excuse me.'

She glided across to the door. She was just in time. A little figure in long white petticoats crashed against her legs with sufficient force to send her staggering back into the sickroom.

Ellen felt Jemmy start as he spotted the stranger in the bed. Instantly his head tilted upwards, presenting a cherubic face to his mother. Chubby arms stretched up.

'Up, up, Mamma — please,' he begged, drawling the last word in a way that demonstrated that, young though he was, he had learnt its power.

Ellen scooped up her son, but shook her head.

'Have you been a naughty boy and run away from Maggie again?' she asked, though not as severely as she might have done.

As if he knew exactly how to manipulate her heartstrings, Jemmy buried his head on her shoulder, apparently deeply ashamed of what he had done. A fierce wave of maternal love swept over Ellen. Of all the little legacies James had left her, this was the most precious and the most vulnerable. The very possibility that Jemmy might have gone toppling backwards down the stairs made her feel nauseous.

'I take it this is your son, Mrs Fairfax?' Robert Lester's voice roused her.

'Yes, this is James — or Jemmy, to distinguish him from his father,' Ellen replied, stroking her son's head. 'Say good morning to Mr Lester, Jemmy.'

'G' morning, Misty Lesty,' Jemmy parroted obediently. And then he spoilt the effect by adding, 'Why's you till in bed?'

'Mr Lester has been ill. Remember when you were ill last winter and stayed in bed all day?'

Jemmy nodded emphatically, but a heavier tread upon the stairs interrupted the conversation.

'Oh, there you are,' Maggie mock-grumbled, eyeing Jemmy as she entered the sickroom with the breakfast tray. 'Got away from me again — as slippery as an eel and as sly as a fox, that one. I need eyes in the back of my head.'

It was not that Jemmy was intentionally naughty, Ellen knew. He was simply too full of life and adventurousness and, at not yet three, he was not old enough to realise when he put himself in danger.

38

'Perhaps I should take him for his walk while Mr Lester has his breakfast,' Ellen suggested. As soon as she had closed the door behind them, she added, 'I thought I might go to the Grange to talk to my cousin.'

Maggie didn't ask why such a visit might be sensible. There were few, if any, secrets between mistress and maid. They'd been through a great deal together. Maggie had nursed Ellen in childbed and braved the Atlantic Ocean with her and the whining, puking baby, so Ellen might spend what time she could with her husband. Nor had Maggie deserted them after James's death, despite having her own sorrows.

'I'll get him wrapped up,' Maggie began, but before she had finished the sentence, there was an imperious rap at the front door.

'Who on earth can that be?' Ellen exclaimed, annoyed. The knock was repeated. 'Go, go.' She flapped her free hand at Maggie. 'Get rid of whoever it is as quickly as possible.'

Maggie did not need to be asked twice. More nimbly than might have been expected from a woman of her comfortable girth, she trotted down the stairs. But notwithstanding her speed, she could not reach the door before the third and most imperious knock of all.

Ellen did not move from her spot on the landing. Her heart was thudding almost as insistently as the knuckles of the caller. She knew only one person who announced herself so determinedly; and Mrs Marley, the parson's wife, was the very last person she wished to see.

Even if she had not had a strange man in the spare bedroom, she would not have been keen to receive one of Mrs Marley's visits, but local society being so close-knit, it was both difficult and imprudent to avoid her.

Silently Ellen prayed for a miracle. But sure enough, Maggie's excuses were cut ruthlessly short.

'Nonsense. I won't take a moment of her time. Be so good as to tell your mistress that I am here on Very Important Business.'

Ellen smiled wryly, hearing the capital letters in the deep, forceful voice.

And then Jemmy squirmed in her arms and drawled preternaturally loudly, 'Mamma?'

Ellen shut her eyes. But she knew she had no choice. She would have to go downstairs and face the consequences of her attempted evasion.

3

Taking a deep breath, Ellen stepped onto the staircase, still carrying Jemmy on her hip, though he was growing restless after being still for all of five minutes. The heads of both women in the hall shot upwards at the sound of her steps.

'There.' Mrs Marley hurled a triumphant look at Maggie. 'I knew you'd see me, my dear Mrs Fairfax.'

Her voice boomed more than ever. Ellen couldn't help hoping Mr Lester would recognise her voice and lie low until the greatest gossip in the parish had departed. Otherwise there was no saying what damage this might do to Ellen's reputation.

'Ah, Mrs Marley, I had no idea you were here,' Ellen lied hastily as she pattered down the stairs. 'Say good morning to Mrs Marley, Jemmy.'

'G' morning, Missy Marley,' Jemmy repeated. Then, as an afterthought, he added, 'Misty Lesty till in bed, 'cos he's sick.'

For half a minute, Ellen felt she could not breathe. Her mind whirred. Was it better to laugh away Jemmy's words as meaningless childish prattle, or try to explain?

Mrs Marley bestowed a wintry smile upon mother and son.

'What a charming child,' she said, in tones that implied that she preferred children to be out of sight and earshot whenever possible. 'Perhaps we could discuss the matter I have come about? I have several more calls to pay this morning.'

She hadn't listened to Jemmy's words, or if she had, hadn't understood them. The revelation struck Ellen like a shaft of lightning. Never before had she been so grateful that her son's diction was not yet clear enough to be easily comprehensible, except to those who knew him well.

'Of course,' she replied to the parson's wife. 'Won't you step into the parlour? Perhaps you could fetch some hot water for some tea, Maggie?'

She gave the maid a reassuring smile behind Mrs Marley's back, but Maggie still looked disgruntled at having come off the worse in the dispute at the door. She bobbed her head in assent, removed Jemmy from his mother's arms and cast a meaningful glance towards Robert Lester's bedroom.

But it had occurred to Ellen that Mrs Marley might be put to good use. Robert Lester was eager to find his family, and who better to help locate them than Mrs Marley, who knew everything of importance and much that was trivial about her neighbours? Maybe once she had transacted whatever business had brought her here, Mrs Marley might be induced to talk about the previous occupants of the steward's house. Ellen knew her sudden interest was unlikely to cause any suspicion in Mrs Marley's mind, since she would assume Ellen's questions were motivated by the same kind of curiosity as her own.

Ellen wished she could have exchanged a few private words with Maggie, but there simply wasn't time. Mrs Marley needed to have sufficient attention paid to her to keep her happy.

The visitor bustled into the parlour ahead of Ellen, but stopped abruptly halfway between the couch and the most comfortable armchair.

Ellen's heart gave a great lurch, then seemed to stop altogether. Maggie had lit the fire on the hearth, but that was all she had had time to do this morning. Mrs Marley had probably not yet noticed the gentleman's stock draped over the arm of the couch. Instead her eyes were fixed ominously on the single, mud-spattered boot on the hearthrug.

Slowly, she swung round to fix Ellen with a meaningful look, drawing in her mouth so that it almost vanished amid the soft folds of sagging flesh.

'Ah, you find me at sixes and sevens today.' Ellen put on her most vivid smile. 'I've — I've been trying to sort out a few of my husband's things. I can't think what's become of the other boot . . . '

She rustled past her unexpected visitor, picking up the stock in passing behind the shield of her full black petticoats. She stuffed it into her pocket as she stooped to retrieve the boot.

'Do sit down. I won't be a moment.'

She whisked out of the door, not daring to look at Mrs Marley's expression. Ellen's first instinct was to leave the boot in the hall, but a second's reflection told her it would be safer by far to have it where no other chance visitors might inadvertently catch sight of it. She scurried along the short passage to the kitchen.

Maggie started as the door sprang open. Then she saw what her mistress was carrying.

'Oh Lord, I clean forgot.'

'So did I. Never mind. I told Mrs

Marley it was my husband's,' Ellen whispered, 'though I'm not sure that that explains why it should be covered with fresh mud.'

She left the boot in the kitchen and flew back to the parlour, though she knew full well it was undignified for a lady to run, and especially so for a widow. Mrs Marley did not chide her out loud, but there was no need. Her expression spoke more loudly than words.

'I'm so sorry for the delay, Mrs Marley. Now, what can I do for you?'

Ellen sat down opposite her visitor, trying not to pant too obviously and surreptitiously throwing glances about the room in case there was any other incriminating evidence she had forgotten. Fortunately she had had the foresight to take the second crutch upstairs the previous evening, because she could not think how she would have explained its presence in her parlour.

It occurred to her much too late that she ought to have feigned tearfulness rather than cheerfulness if she really had been sorting through James's effects. Mrs Marley would now tell the whole parish that Mrs Fairfax was flighty and had not loved her husband one jot.

Ellen blinked back a sudden tear and forced herself to concentrate on what Mrs Marley had to say.

'Well,' the parson's wife announced, 'it has been decided among the chief ladies of the parish that we ought to have a subscription concert for the benefit of the widows and fatherless children of local soldiers who have lost their lives in America.'

Something about the tone of Mrs Marley's voice told Ellen that this was her idea and that she intended to see that it was organised just as she judged best.

'A very laudable cause,' Ellen began, but was cut short.

'Yes, I thought you might say that,' Mrs Marley said, with a shrewd look at the younger woman. 'I suppose I can count on your assistance, given your late husband's profession?'

'Of course.'

Ellen managed to retain a smile while simultaneously wondering if it was really possible for anyone to be so unintentionally tactless. Could there be an element of malice beneath the woman's words? Or was it an attempt to catch Ellen out, if Mrs Marley suspected that she was not who she purported to be?

Ellen knew how the minds of people worked in closed communities. Despite her connection with the new squire — or perhaps because of it — she was sure there must have been gossip about her, perhaps suggesting that rather than being Mr Longridge's impoverished cousin, she was in fact his long-standing mistress and that her dead husband was a convenient fiction to explain the existence of Jemmy.

She listened patiently while Mrs Marley expounded on the plans she had already made. All that was required of

Ellen was to make noncommittal noises here and there, which her visitor clearly interpreted as approval.

Not even the arrival of Maggie with the tea tray could interrupt Mrs Marley now that she was in full flow. Mistress and maid exchanged wry looks before Maggie withdrew to take Jemmy for his morning walk.

'I'll do what I can,' Ellen promised for what felt like the thirtieth time, though she was conscious of how frugally she was forced to live. There was little money to spare for charity, and she had not had time to practise her music for many a long year and therefore couldn't offer to take part in the concert. In any case, her musical education had been distinctly haphazard.

'Splendid, splendid.' But Mrs Marley looked distracted. 'And perhaps you could use your influence with Mr Longridge to engage his patronage for our little venture?'

Ah, now we come to the real reason

for your call, Ellen thought. 'Certainly,' she replied, 'but I don't foresee any difficulties. My cousin takes his duties as lord of the manor very seriously.'

This was enough to set Mrs Marley off into a gush of praise for the new squire — exactly the effect Ellen had been aiming for, since she hoped it would afford her an opportunity to ask what she really wanted to know.

'I'm only too well aware of my cousin's generosity, having been a beneficiary of it myself,' she said, as soon as she could get a word in edgewise. 'I can't help wondering, though, about the family that lived in this house before me. They seem to have left such a quantity of furniture behind. Wasn't this formerly the steward's house?'

Mrs Marley pursed her mouth and gave her the look that by now Ellen had come to recognise meant that the parson's wife had a great deal to say and was only pausing to marshal her thoughts.

'Indeed it was, but even after Mr Lester's death — he fell from his horse in the course of his duties — old Mr Longridge allowed his widow and daughter to stay on. Oh, there was a son as well, but he was in the army and so could not provide a home for his mother or sister.'

Just smile and nod and try to find the right probing question, Ellen told herself.

'So I suppose when old Mr Longridge died, they were obliged to make other arrangements?' she asked in as compassionate a tone as she could muster.

'Oh no, goodness gracious, no. That's the thing. Mr Longridge left a clause in his will that Mrs Lester and her daughter were to be allowed to dwell here as long as was necessary to them. They even say that on his very deathbed, he begged his heir to honour the agreement, and . . . '

For once Mrs Marley stumbled over her words and reddened, conscious of

Ellen's connection with the new squire whose honour she was apparently questioning.

'Not that there was the slightest whisper to suggest young Mr Longridge tried to evict Mrs Lester and her daughter. Far from it. Mrs Lester always spoke with a great deal of gratitude for the kindness he had shown them since becoming squire,' Mrs Marley ran on. 'There was even some foolish talk about an attachment between Mr Longridge and Miss Lester. Of course there was no question of that — the inequality of the match forbade it, even if Mr Longridge hadn't had his eye on a much more suitable match.'

Ellen pricked up her ears at this. It was true she had not lived in the steward's cottage for more than a few weeks, but in that time she had not seen or heard anything to suggest that her cousin was contemplating marriage, suitable or otherwise. Indeed, he had often seemed morose and preoccupied when he was at home — and he had been frequently absent for days at a time.

Still, Ellen couldn't help feeling they were drifting from the subject. But while she was trying to find a way to steer Mrs Marley back in the right direction, the parson's wife forestalled her.

' . . . and then all of a sudden, in the middle of the night, they were both gone, mother and daughter, with no more luggage than they could carry.'

Ellen found her heart pounding. A moonlit flit? Surely that could only mean one thing — that Mrs Lester had mired herself so badly in debt that this was the only solution she could find to her troubles, short of declaring herself bankrupt or allowing herself to be thrown into debtors' prison.

But for the sake of the wounded officer upstairs, Ellen was reluctant to plant this suspicion in Mrs Marley's mind. Besides which, she knew from experience that there were times when the older woman's words could not be taken *too* literally.

'So, where did they go?' Ellen asked.

But the parson's wife shook her head.

'I've already *told* you,' she said with the exasperated patience of a parent talking to a troublesome child. 'Nobody knows. They didn't leave an address or tell anyone when or where they were going. There was some talk that they'd taken places on the London stagecoach, but nobody knows anything else. *And* as far as I am aware, they have never sent word about where the remainder of their possessions should be forwarded.'

A chill trickled down Ellen's spine. Instinct told her that there were only two explanations for such a flight, cutting off all ties and abandoning all possessions. Either Mrs Lester and her daughter were so terrified of something or someone that this complete breach with their past was necessary — or else, even more sinisterly, neither of them was still alive and therefore had no further need of their belongings.

'Surely they must have left word with somebody,' Ellen urged. 'Did you not say there was a son too? Even if they were fleeing from some other trouble, or were called away suddenly by a relative, they would leave word so that the younger Mr Lester could find them.'

Ellen's voice trailed away. Had she betrayed her secret? Mrs Marley was staring at her with such startlingly sepulchral eyes that it unnerved her. As if she had just said something sacrilegious in church, Ellen thought.

'But Robert Lester is *dead*,' the parson's wife said. 'Surely you knew that? They received a letter — oh, some time last winter, I believe it was — to say he'd been gravely wounded and wasn't expected to live more than a few hours, and then they heard nothing more, though they kept hoping it was a mistake for far longer than was wise.'

Mrs Marley sniffed pointedly, as if there was something unchristian in clinging to a faint hope for as long as there was no absolute confirmation of death.

The irony was that while Mrs Lester and her daughter had been worrying and grieving, Robert Lester had been recovering from his injury. Evidently his letters had been lost or delayed amid the chaos of war or on the turbulence of the Atlantic Ocean.

Ellen suppressed a heartfelt groan. She was not looking forward to breaking this news to the stranger upstairs.

★ ★ ★

It was fortunate, Ellen decided, that Mrs Marley was so full of the charitable concert. Otherwise now that she had started to gossip about her husband's parishioners, it might have been extremely difficult to get her to stop.

As it was, it took a gentle hint from Ellen to remind the parson's wife that she had a number of other calls to pay before the morning was over. Relieved, Ellen rose too to escort her visitor to the front door.

Her relief was short-lived. Almost as soon as she set foot in the hall, Ellen caught the sound of a cautious creak on the stairs. Her heart plummeted and momentarily she squeezed her eyes shut.

Dear God, not that. Anything but that. Please let it be my imagination and nothing more.

Cautiously she glanced at the parson's wife and her heart sank still further. Mrs Marley had already twisted her head towards the staircase. No words were necessary. Her expression — eyes and mouth round — revealed to Ellen that she had been caught out.

Unwillingly, she turned. Mr Lester was near the top of the stairs, clinging convulsively to his crutches. He had been pale when Ellen first looked up, but now he flushed, clearly mortified at having made his appearance at such an inopportune moment. It must have added to his embarrassment that his injury prevented him from either coming forward swiftly and boldly or from beating a hasty retreat.

For his sake, Ellen rallied with an effort.

'Ah, Mrs Marley,' she said, 'I believe you are acquainted with our resident ghost, Mr Robert Lester.'

4

'I'm really sorry . . . '

'I cannot apologise enough . . . '

They both began to speak as soon as the door had closed. Ellen couldn't help ducking her head and giggling self-consciously under Robert Lester's apologetic gaze.

Charity concert or not, it had been no easy matter to persuade Mrs Marley to leave, now that she thought she had stumbled upon a scandal. Between them, Ellen and Robert Lester had tried to explain the circumstances of his arrival. But Ellen had the impression that, no matter what they said, Mrs Marley would draw her own conclusions about what had occurred the previous night — and would no doubt spread the benefit of her insight throughout her husband's parish. The only useful thing that had emerged from the encounter was that Mrs Marley had confirmed that Robert Lester was indeed who he claimed to be.

Jemmy had added to the confusion by returning from his walk with Maggie at precisely the wrong moment. He had run to his mother, eager to tell her what he had seen, but quickly grew frustrated because nobody had leisure to listen to him. He had not protested much, but had butted his head against his mother's shoulder when she picked him up. It was only a small gesture and hadn't even hurt, but Ellen saw Mrs Marley's lips tighten in disapproval.

'Perhaps we ought to go into the parlour,' Ellen suggested now, seeing the strain in her patient's face from making his cautious way down the stairs. 'We can talk just as easily seated as we can standing.'

All this while Jemmy had been viewing the stranger dubiously from the curve of his mother's shoulder where he had nestled his head. But as Ellen crossed the hall to open the parlour door, Jemmy stretched out a venturesome finger to poke Robert Lester's sleeve.

'Papa's coat,' he announced.

Ellen did not know whether to laugh, cry or praise her son for his cleverness.

'Well, no, not quite, darling,' she said, trying to keep her voice steady. 'But Papa did have a very similar coat.'

James's dress coat still hung in a clothes-press upstairs. Once, as a joke, Maggie had dressed Jemmy up in it and placed James's tricorn on his son's head — another occasion when Ellen had not known whether to laugh or to cry. The most tragic thing was that Jemmy had been far too young when his father died to have any memories of him.

But she had a duty to carry out. Suppressing a sigh, Ellen attempted to set Jemmy down, but he clung to her like a monkey.

'Please, Jemmy, run along with Maggie now and I'll talk to you later,' Ellen said. 'There's something very

important I must tell Mr Lester first.'
Ellen saw her son's lower lip jut out and
his eyes brim. It smote her heart.

'Please, Mrs Fairfax, I'm sure my
business can wait,' Robert Lester
intervened. 'Let Jemmy tell you all
about his walk. Indeed, I should very
much like to hear it myself, if I may.'

Ellen threw him a grateful look. She
knew she ought to demur, but his
words sounded so sincere and chimed
so precisely with her urges as a mother
that she could not bring herself to draw
the process out too long.

'Are you sure?' she asked. 'When
Jemmy tells me his stories, it can
sometimes take a while.'

'I'm sure,' Robert Lester replied
firmly.

Ellen led the way into the parlour.
Robert Lester lowered himself into one
of the armchairs by the fire, since it was
higher than the couch, and propped his
crutches alongside. Ellen meanwhile
perched on the edge of the couch with
her son.

She was not sure how much of Jemmy's account of seeing a robin singing on a bare branch Robert Lester understood, since even she had difficulty in keeping up with the rapidity of Jemmy's imperfectly formed words. Nonetheless, the injured officer said, 'Really?' and 'What else did you see?' in all the right places with the right amount of enthusiasm. Jemmy blossomed and seemed to grow before her eyes. He even squirmed out of her lap and ran across to Robert Lester's chair, so he could put his hands on the soldier's good knee and peer up into his face while he gabbled on about the first lambs in the fields, before demonstrating how they had been gambolling.

Ellen couldn't help laughing and as she glanced up, she met the full force of Robert Lester's smile. Something seemed to fizzle and crackle in the air. Everything stood still. All that existed was that smiling face with eyes full of affection for her fatherless son.

Belatedly, Ellen averted her face. In

this homely atmosphere, she had almost succeeded in forgetting that Mr Lester was a virtual stranger and, moreover, someone whom she had a duty to inform of a painful truth.

'Well, Jemmy, if you are done, I think it's time you went to find Maggie in the kitchen and had your glass of milk,' Ellen suggested.

This time Jemmy made no protest, though after he had reached the door he felt obliged to dash back to his mother for one last kiss before he retreated from the room. In the silence that followed his exit, the two adults heard his steps pattering down the short passage and his voice calling out to Maggie.

'You have a handsome and charming son, Mrs Fairfax,' Robert Lester remarked.

'Thank you. He is the most precious thing in the world to me.'

'I can imagine.'

Can you? Really? But Ellen bit back the words. This stranger could not be expected to know all she had done to keep her son, or that she still had nightmares that his grandfather might discover where she had hidden him and descend upon them with all the power of wealth and respectability to prise Jemmy away from her.

'I should like to apologise again for coming downstairs so inopportunely,' Robert Lester said. 'I heard the door and assumed your visitor must have gone.'

Ellen smiled wryly. 'Think nothing of it,' she said. 'What possible harm can a ghost do to a lady's reputation?' She hoped there had not been the slightest hint of reproach in her voice.

'Why do you keep calling me a ghost?'

It was the question she dreaded most.

'Because — I'm sorry to have to tell you this, but — the whole parish seems to believe you died of your injuries last winter.'

He took a moment to digest this.

'My mother and sister too?'

'Yes. At least, I assume so. Mrs Marley said they clung on to hope for as long as they could, but when no word arrived from America . . . ' She shrugged and uselessly added again, 'I'm very sorry.'

There was a long silence, broken only by a rustle as the half-burnt kindling subsided on the hearth.

'Yes, well, it's nobody's fault. Vagaries of the post, especially in a time of war,' he said, trying to sound brisk. 'It will be all the more of a surprise for them to find I am still alive when I do find them.'

Ellen could see that he had convinced himself that this would be a straightforward process — a matter of asking a friend or perhaps the landlord for a forwarding address.

'Of course you're right,' she said, 'but there's something more that Mrs Marley told me, something you ought to know.'

★　★　★

Even before he heard Ellen Fairfax's tale about the disappearance of his family, it had been clear to Robert that he ought not to stay any longer under her roof. It was almost certainly too late to prevent Mrs Marley from broadcasting the news of his presence at the steward's house throughout the parish. But the longer he stayed, the more the rumours would grow.

Now, though, he had another incentive to go — the necessity of beginning his search for his family. His first port of call must be the village of Blidworth. If he could not glean the slightest clue there, he would have to return to Mansfield. Two grown women could not vanish into thin air. Someone somewhere must know something.

Ellen Fairfax understood his motives, but she questioned him closely about whether he still felt feverish. She even offered to send Maggie to the Grange with a note to ask if they might borrow a carriage or a horse, but Robert refused as politely as he could. It would have been different if the old squire, whom Robert had known since boyhood, had still been alive. But he could not ask such a favour from a stranger.

Besides, Robert did not quite trust the younger Mr Longridge. He did not want to say anything to Ellen Fairfax, since she was clearly grateful to her cousin for providing her with shelter, but Robert could not help suspecting that Mr Philip Longridge might know more about the disappearance of the late steward's widow and daughter than he was letting on. All Robert wanted was to glean a little more information from an impartial source before confronting the master of the Grange.

'It isn't far to Blidworth,' he assured his hostess, 'and the weather is perfect for a walk.'

The storm had exhausted itself and washed the sky to the soft, pale blue of a butterfly's wing.

'The roads will still be damp,' Ellen Fairfax objected. 'At least let Maggie accompany you. She has a few errands to run in the village in any case.'

Reluctantly Robert agreed to this, partly because he was concerned about the possibility that he might slip or get stuck in the mud on the little-used track, and partly because he was still a little light-headed after the previous night's fever, though he would not have admitted it in a million years.

There was one further incident that strengthened his resolve to go. While he was donning his newly polished boot, crumpled stock and tricorn and Maggie put on her red cloak and a pair of pattens to protect her shoes, there was a rap at the door. Ellen Fairfax answered it herself and returned a minute later carrying a letter.

'I believe this is yours,' she said, holding it out to him.

For a second Robert did not understand. Then he recognised the writing on the covering sheet as his own. It was the letter he had sent from Portsmouth, warning his mother of his imminent arrival.

As Ellen Fairfax had warned, the ground was still sodden. Every twig and newly unfurled leaf sparkled with droplets to splatter the unwary. At first it was a largely silent trudge across the rolling countryside, past woodland and farmland, until Robert hit upon the brilliant idea of praising Mrs Fairfax's kindness and resourcefulness.

Maggie's face lit up. 'Oh, aye, she's resourceful right enough,' she said. 'She'd have need to be an' all, what with the life she's led. Daughter of the regiment, as well as married into it. So was I, if you come to that, 'cept her husband was a captain and mine a sergeant. Took her under my wing a bit, after her mother died when she was fourteen.'

A very vulnerable age for a girl to be left motherless, Robert thought. Especially a girl surrounded by so many men and having no settled home.

'I've always said it's a hard enough

life in the army for the men, but it's worse for the wives and children,' he said.

'Bad enough in peacetime and worse in war,' Maggie agreed. 'But it's all she'd ever known, with her father being a colonel. He married late in life and died just a few months after her marriage, as if he'd been waiting to see her settled before he let go.'

'I'm sure you did your best to comfort her,' Robert suggested.

Maggie reddened. 'Aye, well,' she mumbled, 'I never did have any children of my own — not that I'm old enough to be Miss Ellen's mother, mind, but ... ' She finished the sentence with a shrug. 'Course, it was her husband she turned to most of all. Quite heartbroken when she had to stay behind when he was posted to America, on account of she was expecting the little one. Terrified she might never see him again. As soon as the baby was big enough to stand the journey, we set sail directly for New York. Never seen a

72

couple more overjoyed to see one another.'

She smiled wistfully, then sighed. 'Dead within a year he was, of course, but Mrs Fairfax's always said she was lucky to have that last year with him, when he could so easily have died at Breed's Hill like my Harry did, before we'd even set foot on the ship.'

'Oh.' The words had been spoken so matter-of-factly, they took Robert's breath away. He rallied with an effort. 'I'm sorry for your loss.'

Maggie dipped her head in acknowledgement, and for some minutes they went on in silence. Robert felt he could not probe any deeper. He had known several women in precisely her predicament.

Hitherto, the road had been easy, sloping gently downwards. Now Robert braced himself for the hill ahead. The village lay beyond it, straggling along the road that wove through yet another valley and up yet another hillside.

'A real love match it was and all,

between Miss Ellen and the captain,' Maggie went on unexpectedly, turning to face him as if she thought he was likely to dispute it. 'His folks thought they were a deal too high for him to be marrying a penniless colonel's daughter, but the captain insisted and he got his own way. I daresay he and the younger Mrs Fairfax were a deal happier living hand-to-mouth with the regiment than his parents, for all their grand mansion.' Maggie uttered a contemptuous sniff.

'I hadn't realised Captain Fairfax's family were wealthy,' Robert remarked cautiously.

'Still are — and use their money as a weapon too.'

Robert was not quite sure what to make of this. 'I suppose it's because they disapprove of Mrs Fairfax that her late husband's family refused to help her financially?' he suggested.

Maggie shook her head and smiled once more in her cynical fashion. 'No, no, t'other way round. The Fairfaxes have far too strong a sense of *duty* to neglect appearances like that.' She pushed her basket further up her arm. 'They're willing enough to *help*, but only on their own terms.'

'Oh?'

'It's them that Miss Ellen's hiding from here. When she got back from America, they absolutely insisted that she and the little one should go and live with them in that great tomb of a place they have. They were so desperate to have her there that they let her keep me on as Jemmy's nurse — not good enough to be a lady's maid, see.'

With her plain-spoken common sense, Robert found it hard to imagine Maggie would ever have fitted in at the grand household she had hinted at.

'They stifled the fire and life out of Miss Ellen, though I daresay she might have stuck it out if that had been all. No, she felt she had to leave on account of her little boy. She knew how unhappy her husband had been as a boy because he'd told her; and when she saw they wanted to bring up her Jemmy just as severely as they had their own son she rebelled, packed up her traps and decamped with me and the little one in tow. Better a dinner of herbs where love is — and all that.'

'I see.'

Robert couldn't help admiring Ellen's courage in striking out on her own for the sake of her son's welfare, when prudence might have dictated that she ought to learn to submit to the will of her late husband's parents.

But there was no time for any more conversation. The first houses of the village had come into sight as they crested the ridge. Robert was struck by how timeless and unchanged it seemed, with its weathered row of stone houses and the little grey church with its square tower, set near the top of the slope.

Soon he would be within sight of the modest inn in which he was pretty certain he would be able to hire a room for a few days, until he decided where best to start searching for his family.

That was the disadvantage of having a travelling companion, he mused. If he had come alone, he would have had plenty of time to think out his plan of action. Now all he could do was play things by ear.

★ ★ ★

The hours that followed his parting from Maggie proved to be more of an ordeal than Robert had anticipated. In contrast with Mansfield, where he had contrived to pass unrecognised, it seemed to him that the entire village erupted from the houses and workshops to come and stare at him in wonder, or offer to stand him a jug of ale at the inn.

Mrs Marley had clearly done her work. Everybody seemed to know that the late steward's son had, as it were, come back from his grave — a miracle in itself, even without being coupled with the mystery surrounding the disappearance of his family.

It was wholly inevitable that, sooner rather than later, Robert found himself seated in the chimney corner of the inn, pewter tankard before him on the scratched tabletop, while dozens of voices buzzed around him asking questions, passing on news, and marvelling at his return.

It was easy enough for Robert to ask, apparently completely innocently, about the character of the new owner of the Grange. The death of old Mr Longridge and his nephew's arrival to take charge of his inheritance were inevitably the most important events that had happened in such a small place. But Robert could not overlook the uneasy glances that were exchanged by the more sober villagers at his question.

'Oh, he seems a fair enough master so far,' the blacksmith replied cautiously. 'Not much of a one for talking, but then, there's not many gentlemen that would pass the time of day with the likes of us, unless he had some special business wi' us.'

'Ah, it's allus the quiet ones you've to watch,' one of the older labourers chimed in, much to the alarm of some of his neighbours. They tried to shush him, but the old man was too far-gone with drink to pay them heed. 'He's a deep one, that 'un, you mark my words. Knows a trick or two, I warrant.'

There was no mistaking the meaningful look he cast at Robert.

'What do you mean by that?' Robert decided it might be as well to take the bait.

'Pay no heed to him,' one of the other villagers urged. 'Allus too loose a tongue on him when he's had a drop too many. Get himsen thrown out of that hovel of his one of these days.'

But even this veiled warning didn't quieten the old man.

'Oh, is that so, is it? Are you so afeared of the new squire that you'll let yon poor crippled lad stay in ignorance about what happened to his ma and sister?'

'Nay, you know nowt more than any of the rest of us.'

'Oh, and don't I, though? On the day before they disappeared, I chanced to be passing by their house on my way back from Mansfield market, and who should I see but the fine young squire quarrelling with Miss Polly! Had hold of her wrist and all, though he let go sharpish when he caught sight of me. She ran off into the house as quick as a flash, and nobody's seen hide nor hair of her or her mother from that day to this.'

5

Dinner had not even been served yet and already Ellen was sorry she had accepted the invitation to spend the evening at the Grange.

Her cousin Philip had called at the steward's house on his way home, not even dismounting from his horse to issue his invitation, since he had happened to catch her as she was returning from a walk designed to tire Jemmy's little legs and ensure he slept soundly.

'You will come, won't you, Ellen?' She had sensed a suppressed urgency behind his usually clipped delivery. 'Caroline arrived unexpectedly last night with her usual entourage.'

'Caroline? What can have brought her back so soon?'

Caroline was Philip's married older sister. Ellen knew that she had taken it upon herself to descend on the Grange shortly after Philip inherited it on the pretext that, as a bachelor, her brother must be in want of a female hand to set the household in order.

Philip pulled a rueful face. 'Oh, you know Caroline,' he said. 'I daresay she thinks that thanks to my mismanagement the house must have fallen to rack and ruin in the three months she has been absent.'

But it hadn't taken Ellen ten minutes since arriving at the Grange to discover that Caroline had another motive entirely. In addition to her somewhat plump, passive husband Jonathan, Caroline had also brought her husband's ward, an eighteen-year-old heiress by the name of Amelia D'Arcy.

There was no doubt in Ellen's mind that Caroline was doing her utmost to draw her brother's attention to all of Miss D'Arcy's accomplishments and good qualities. What was less obvious was whether Philip was behaving in such an abrupt, distracted manner because he was unaware of what his sister was doing, or because he understood her motives only too well.

If that had been all, Ellen might have spent an amusing evening, watching the various stratagems and manoeuvrings of her cousins. Unfortunately Mrs Marley had called at the Grange that morning after her visit to the steward's house. ('On the chance of finding Mr Longridge at home,' the parson's wife had explained to Ellen.)

Instead she had encountered Caroline Hume, who had instantly assumed the mantle of hostess and invited the parson and his wife to dine at the Grange that evening. The result was that Ellen had had to endure a string of questions and speculations about the unexpected return of Lieutenant Lester, as if Mrs Marley thought that if she persisted long enough, Ellen might let slip some incriminating detail about her connection with the revenant.

Caroline and Miss D'Arcy also seemed fascinated by the subject, particularly as, Ellen gathered, their previous visit had coincided with the disappearance of Mrs and Miss Lester. Caroline even asked Mrs Marley several times if she was absolutely certain that the injured soldier was truly Robert Lester and not some impostor.

But while the group as a whole discussed the subject of the Lesters with a good deal of vigour, Ellen noticed Philip had sunk even deeper into his habitual silence.

'What do you think, Philip?' Caroline appealed to her brother.

'About what?'

'About the return of Mr Lester,' Caroline replied, a shade impatiently. 'I mean — what is to be done about him?'

'Done? I am sure he is perfectly capable of making up his own mind about what he wishes to do next.'

'Yes, but now that his family has gone and he can no longer follow his profession, he is bound to need help of one kind or another.' It was obvious that Caroline was growing exasperated by her brother's refusal to understand her.

If anything, Philip's expression seemed to grow even more closed. 'I plan to call on him tomorrow and offer him my assistance, if that is what you are hinting at,' Philip replied in a way that suggested that he intended to say no more on the subject, no matter how much she might goad him.

'Oh.' Caroline was visibly uneasy, but Ellen couldn't work out why. 'Well, of course, if you think it is necessary . . . ' She trailed away and then with renewed vigour launched into another subject. 'You must tell me more about this benefit concert you are arranging, Mrs Marley. My own singing and playing days are over, of course, but if we are still here when it takes place, Miss D'Arcy might be persuaded to take part.'

'I'm not sure — ' Amelia D'Arcy

began, but her guardian's wife over-ruled her.

'Now, now, you must not be too modest or hide your light under a bushel. I know you did not want to go to London this year out of respect for your dear departed father, but you cannot be allowed to pine away for want of company. And this is such a worthwhile cause.'

The torrent of words was brought to an abrupt halt. A thunderous rap at the front door seemed to echo through the whole house.

'Who the deuce can that be?' Philip muttered before turning his glance on his sister. 'You haven't invited anyone else to join us tonight, have you, Caroline, and then neglected to inform me?'

'Oh!' Caroline exclaimed, affronted. She cast an anxious look at the Marleys, just in case Philip had succeeded in insulting them too by implying that their presence was unwelcome.

But Mr Marley — a pale, insignificant man with a cadaverous face and a voice that failed to carry, even in a small parish church — looked unmoved by Philip's words, while his wife was evidently too interested in the origin of the vigorous drum-roll of a knock to have had time to consider the implications of the new squire's words.

'Mr Robert Lester to see you, sir,' a maid announced. She licked her lips nervously. 'I told him you were engaged, but he was very insistent.'

Ellen saw her cousin's jaw clench and unclench.

'No, no, it's all right. Of course I must see him.' He rose from his seat, but Ellen could see his reluctance. 'Show him into the — '

But before he could complete his sentence, a second figure appeared in the doorway behind the servant.

* * *

Ellen was struck by the grimness of Robert Lester's expression. His eyes instinctively found Philip's face.

'Mr Longridge, I presume,' he said, dodging past the maid before anyone could stop him. 'I'm sorry to intrude, but you will understand, I hope, how anxious I am about the welfare of my family.'

'Quite understandable,' Philip replied in studiedly neutral tones. 'And naturally if I can be of any use to you in your search . . . '

Suddenly the former soldier lurched closer to the squire, his dark eyes boring into the other man's face.

'Ah, it is interesting that you should say that,' he said, 'because I have it on good authority that you were seen quarrelling with my sister — and holding her against her will — on the day before she disappeared.'

Ellen felt a frisson rush through the drawing room as Caroline and Mrs Marley pricked up their ears.

But Ellen's gaze was riveted, like Robert's, to Philip's face. He had turned dark red, his eyes emitting sparks, his jaw more clenched than ever. Ellen found herself questioning what emotion was uppermost in his breast. Outrage at a preposterous accusation? Or guilt at being caught out?

'Take care what you insinuate about me,' he growled. 'My intentions towards Miss Lester have never been other than honourable.'

The iciness of Philip's voice told Ellen how angry he was at being attacked like this in his own home, and in front of guests too. Robert Lester could not have chosen a less promising way to approach her cousin if he hoped for an honest and open answer.

Someone had to intervene and surely it was better that she should do it herself, rather than leave it to somebody more tactless, like Caroline.

'I'm sure Mr Lester meant no disrespect, Philip,' Ellen said, gliding forward to place her hand on her cousin's arm in what appeared to be a gesture of solidarity, though in fact it was intended to act as a restraint on him and a reminder of who else was present in the room. 'When they are upset, people don't always say what they mean.'

She kept her eyes fixed on Robert Lester as she spoke, willing him to back down a little, but her heart sank. He had started at the sound of her voice, which suggested that he had been unaware of her presence until that moment.

But she could see from the change in his expression that he had misinterpreted her gesture in aligning herself with her cousin. No doubt he now regarded her as part of a conspiracy to hush up the true circumstances of his family's disappearance.

'Thank you, Ellen. I understand Mr Lester's position perfectly well,' Philip retorted, his voice still frosty.

Wonderful, Ellen thought. *I try to be useful and manage to alienate both participants in this dispute.*

'As their former landlord, I am also anxious to ascertain that Miss Lester and her mother are in comfortable circumstances,' Philip went on, but there was something unnatural about his tone.

It was obvious from Robert Lester's sceptical look that he did not believe the other man was sincere. Even Ellen felt an inexplicable shudder run down her spine.

'I suppose, then, I can rely on your assistance to locate my family?' Robert drawled, the same disbelieving smile on his lips.

Again Philip flushed. He seemed to be choosing his next words carefully, but as ill luck would have it, Caroline leaped into the breach.

'I don't know why you should think my brother had anything to do with the disappearance of your family,' she said. 'But if it's money you're after . . . '

She got no further.

'Thank you, I am not a beggar yet.' This time there was no disguising the scorn in Robert Lester's voice. 'I would be satisfied with the plain, unvarnished truth.'

Ellen felt the muscles in Philip's arm contract and she tightened her grip, willing him to keep his temper in the face of provocation. She could not help but be a little affronted herself. Philip was her cousin, after all, and she knew that his honesty had never been questioned before. She was almost afraid Philip might forget who his opponent was and challenge him to a duel if the latter did not withdraw the slur.

'The truth?' Philip echoed. 'Is that what you think you got from that drunken sot from the village?'

Ellen saw a flicker of colour in Robert's cheek, which betrayed that Philip had touched upon a sore spot.

'I won't deny that Miss Lester and I did not part on the best of terms,' Philip went on, 'but as far as I am concerned, there was no need for her or her mother to depart as they did. And now, if you have no objection, sir, I'd like you to leave. My guests have been waiting for their dinner quite long enough in my opinion.'

For a long time, the eyes of the two men locked in a silent battle of wills. But Robert Lester must have known he could not win. If he did not back down gracefully while he had the chance, he would be expelled ignominiously as a troublemaker.

'As you wish, sir,' he said, with a curt bow of the head. 'But do not think you have heard the last of this matter.'

And with that, he turned and retraced his steps to the door at which the astonished maid was still standing, her eyes bulging at the extraordinary scene she had just witnessed. Ellen gestured to her and the maid closed the door behind her and presumably showed Robert Lester out.

'Well!' Both Caroline and Mrs Marley exploded at exactly the same moment; and Ellen had a sudden, barely controllable urge to burst into hysterical giggles.

But Philip stemmed the gush of words before it could begin. 'I have no wish to discuss this matter any further. It has taken up too much time already. Now, shall we go in to dinner?'

★ ★ ★

Philip maintained this position for the remainder of the evening. That did not prevent Mrs Marley, Caroline and Amelia D'Arcy from giving free rein to their speculations once the ladies had withdrawn from the dining room to allow the gentlemen to pass the bottle freely around the table.

There was general agreement among the ladies that it was an outrage that someone so low-born — a servant's son, who would *never* have risen to the rank of an officer, and therefore theoretically gentleman, if there hadn't been a war on — could make such insinuations against someone whose place in society was beyond dispute.

'And to suggest my brother could

have anything to do with that girl.' Caroline shuddered expressively. 'An amiable enough creature, I daresay, for one in her sphere of life — but really!' She cast a pointed look at Amelia D'Arcy who, however, seemed not to notice that this spirited defence of Philip's reputation had been undertaken partly for her benefit.

'I should hate it if you got the wrong impression of the state of my brother's morals,' Caroline pressed her point.

'Oh, I am sure that would never happen,' Miss D'Arcy replied, but Ellen could see she was puzzled by all this emphasis on the subject.

Ellen was relieved when the gentlemen joined them and cut the discussion short. She had not had the most comfortable time, with both Caroline and Mrs Marley pressing her to express an opinion on Robert Lester's character and behaviour.

All in all, the evening was not a great success. Ellen could sense the seething of unexpressed words beneath the surface of polite conversation. She was not surprised when Mrs Marley declared that an early departure was necessary because she had a very busy day on the morrow. What she really meant was that she was desperate to vent her feelings to her husband on the carriage ride home.

'I ought to be going too,' Ellen said once the Marleys had departed.

'I suppose we'd better order the carriage for you,' Caroline said, as usual taking on the responsibilities for managing the household.

Ellen had walked up to the Grange by daylight and had not given much thought to how she should make her way home again.

'Really, there is no need. I am not afraid of walking and it seems a bright, clear night. If I could borrow a lantern . . . '

Ellen's words were cut short by a scandalised cry from Caroline. 'Walk? Alone? At this hour? I won't hear of it. Tell her this is madness, Philip.'

'There can't be any danger,' Ellen replied. 'I won't even leave the grounds of the Grange.'

'Oh, but there may be poachers and burglars and who knows what else lurking out there,' Caroline objected, and Ellen saw Amelia D'Arcy's eyes widen at the thought of being in such a lawless place. 'You must at least take a servant with you for protection.'

'I don't see that there is any need for that . . . '

'Philip!'

He gave his sister a measured look. 'I don't see that there is any need for it,' he repeated mildly, 'since I intend to walk Ellen back to her house myself.'

And with that, he ushered Ellen from the room, turning a deaf ear to his sister's protests that he might be in even greater peril to life and limb if they should encounter a poacher or a disgruntled tenant along the way.

'Really, Philip,' Ellen protested once they were safely outdoors, 'I'm perfectly capable of finding my own way home.

There was no need for you to come on my account.'

'Maybe not, but maybe I came on my own account,' Philip replied with his usual curtness.

Suddenly Ellen understood. He knew that as soon as all the guests had departed, perhaps even before Amelia D'Arcy had retired to her room, Caroline would launch an attack on him on the subject of Robert Lester and his sister.

'You cannot avoid Caroline forever,' Ellen said. 'Sooner or later she will try to winkle out of you what you had to say to Miss Lester during that last meeting.'

Ellen's hand was tucked through the crook of her cousin's elbow. She felt the muscles contract in his arm.

'It's a private matter,' he replied stiffly.

'I believe you, and that excuse *might* serve to put off Caroline,' Ellen conceded, 'but forgive me if I say I hardly think Mr Lester will see it that way. Are you absolutely sure that Miss Lester did not give you any indication that she and her mother might have to leave the cottage or where they might go?'

Philip averted his head sharply, though even with a full moon and the lantern he carried, it was too dark for Ellen to make out his expression.

'If I did know where they had gone, do you really think so meanly of my character that you believe I would not have told Mr Lester?'

His tone made Ellen shiver. She thought she detected a quiver of anguish in his words. She felt she was on the brink of a revelation and would have to tread carefully so as not to cause her cousin to clam up again.

'There's something more, isn't there?' she said slowly. 'Something you have not been able to tell anyone, because there is nobody you trust.'

6

For a long time, Ellen thought Philip wouldn't reply. He yanked himself free of her grip and strode a few paces ahead. The March night suddenly felt very chill, though Ellen reminded herself that she had been colder than this before in America, on forced marches and nocturnal evacuations to evade the enemy's vigilance.

'Look, Philip,' she said, softening her tone, 'I don't want to pry or to force your confidence. But you have not been yourself since I arrived in Nottinghamshire. You have been moody and withdrawn and monosyllabic. Whatever secret you are keeping, it is clearly not doing you any good. So if ever you wish to speak to me, you know you can trust me to be discreet. I am not Caroline.'

He did not reply at once, but his head dipped so his chin was almost resting on his breast. Ellen took a few steps closer and reached out to touch his arm. He raised his other hand to rub his forehead, as if he was suddenly very tired and his eyes were smarting.

'Oh, very well,' he burst out. 'If you *must* know, I — I'm in love with Polly Lester. There, now are you satisfied?'

Ellen felt as if she had been caught directly beneath an exploding flare. Suddenly everything was vivid and clear in the minutest detail. She felt she had grasped the situation by instinct long before she could reason everything out fully or put it into words.

'Oh, Philip,' she murmured.

He swung round to face her. 'I meant what I said to Lester,' he insisted fiercely. 'My intentions have always been honourable. I intended to ask Miss Lester to marry me last winter, but then the letter came saying that her brother had been fatally injured. I could not force my attentions on her while she was grieving. I did what I could to help her and her mother and assured them they could stay at the steward's house as long as they wished on the same terms as they had agreed with my uncle. There was no need for them to go.' His anguish could not be hidden now.

'Philip, no one is attacking you,' Ellen said. 'There's need for you to defend yourself so vigorously.' But as she spoke, her mind was ticking. How would Robert Lester react if he knew this? Or Caroline, for that matter?

'I'm sorry, Ellen. I didn't mean . . . ' His murmur died away in a sigh and a shrug.

She decided it was safer to ignore these last words, so as not to embarrass her cousin any further. She still needed to get to the bottom of this matter.

'And what about Miss Lester's feelings?' she probed gently. 'Did she turn down your proposal? Is that why you quarrelled before she left?'

But Philip was shaking his head before she could complete her third question.

'No, I never asked her. Or at least, not in the way I had intended. She had been strange and shy around me for — oh, maybe a week or two before that day. So when I chanced to meet her in the lane on her own, I tried to ask her about it, and . . . ' He swallowed a lump of bile that seemed to choke him.

'And what?' Ellen prompted him.

He looked straight into her eyes all of a sudden. 'She'd heard some vile rumour that I was merely toying with her and intended to keep her as my mistress, while marrying Miss D'Arcy for her fortune. I tried to tell her that it was nonsense, but she wouldn't listen — and then one of the more disreputable labourers from the village happened along. She broke away from me and rushed into the house and, like a fool, I didn't go straight after her and insist on speaking to her, or ask her mother for permission to marry her, because I thought it would be better to wait until we had both calmed down and she was more inclined to listen to me.'

'And you never saw her again?'

'No.'

'But you went after her and tried to find her, didn't you?' Ellen had another flash of insight. 'When you disappear for days at a time without a proper explanation — that's the reason why, isn't it?'

'Yes.'

It was probably also because Caroline suspected this might be the case that she had chosen this moment to come back to the Grange and dangle the young, rich and beautiful Amelia D'Arcy beneath her brother's nose again, Ellen thought. But she kept this theory to herself, not wanting to cause any bad blood between her cousins.

'I meant to tell Lester at least some of this when I called on him tomorrow,' Philip went on after a while, and Ellen could hear the awkwardness of embarrassment in his voice again. 'But I couldn't do it in front of witnesses; and the man was so

104

provoking, so determined to think the worst of me . . . '

'Let me talk to him.' Ellen uttered the words instinctively and regretted them instantly. And yet she could not seem to back down. 'I think he might be more inclined to listen to me.'

'By which you mean you are less likely to lose your temper than I.'

Ellen caught a glimpse of Philip's rueful smile in the moonlight.

'That too,' she replied and he laughed.

'Thank you, Ellen. You've always been a good friend as well as my favourite cousin.'

★ ★ ★

Ellen had had a chance to regret her offer a thousand times over by the time she reached the inn at Blidworth on the following morning.

She had seen the suspicious way in which Robert Lester had regarded her at the Grange. Moreover, it was not quite the done thing for a young widow to seek out an unmarried man, particularly as she knew that gossip about her must already be rife in the village.

That was one of the reasons why she had taken Jemmy with her, as a miniature chaperon. She was almost certain that Robert Lester would be careful not to lose his temper or use immoderate language in front of such a small child.

She had hoped that she might encounter her quarry somewhere along the way. But luck was not on her side. She would have to venture inside the inn and ask after her former patient as casually as she could. There was even a possibility that Robert Lester might have already set out in one direction or another, to make enquiries after his mother and sister.

But Fortune wasn't apparently completely against her. Yes, she was forced to ask the innkeeper for information, but he assured her that Mr Lester had not yet left.

'I'll go and fetch him for you, shall I?' he said, cocking a beady eye at her.

Ellen found herself flushing and wishing she could tell him not to bother, since it was merely a courtesy call.

'If you would be so kind,' she replied instead, with as much dignity as she could muster.

She was forced to wait a good while — long enough for her to become nervous and for Jemmy to grow restless — before she heard the cautious approach of crutches and a wooden leg on the bare wooden staircase.

She took a few steps forward to meet him.

'Mr Lester,' she said softly. 'It was good of you to agree to see me.'

'Not at all,' he replied, but there was a new formality about him. He wasn't going to make this easy for her. And hers was a delicate mission. This was far too public a place for her to speak to him in confidence.

'Jemmy and I are taking a walk; and as we were passing, we thought you might like to join us — didn't we, Jemmy?'

She tried to speak casually, but as Jemmy nodded his head solemnly, she could feel her cheeks growing crimson. Even such an innocent invitation felt a little forward. And if Robert Lester turned it down, could she coax him into changing his mind?

He scrutinised her face, as if looking for clues to her true intentions. But his expression softened as he looked down at Jemmy, half-hidden behind his mother's petticoats.

'I'd be delighted,' Robert Lester replied, though his tone was still guarded.

'Excellent.' She couldn't help smiling with relief, until she caught the innkeeper's wife watching them with a speculative air. The sooner they were away from this place, the better. 'Come along, Jemmy.'

Ellen helped her son clamber over the doorstep and then waited for Robert Lester to join them.

'Which way, Mrs Fairfax?' the latter asked, as he resettled his tricorn hat, which had clipped the lintel.

'I thought perhaps we might go to the Druid Stone. Unless the road is too steep for you?'

It was his turn to flush, clearly annoyed at having attention drawn to his injury.

'I can manage,' he clipped. 'I've not been there since my return. It will be interesting to see if everything is still as I remember it.'

They set off at a moderate pace to accommodate Jemmy's little steps. There were a number of people in the street going about their business, but Ellen felt a little safer speaking here, as long as she kept her voice low.

'There is something I wanted to tell you,' she said.

'I thought that might be the case.'

Ellen pretended to ignore the sarcasm in his voice. 'It concerns your sister,' she went on sweetly. 'But if you are not interested, we might as well part here.'

Her words had the desired effect.

'I apologise, Mrs Fairfax,' Robert Lester replied in a conciliatory tone. 'Do go on.'

Ellen glanced around, then shook her head. 'Not here,' she said.

Robert Lester gave her a quizzical look. 'Are you punishing me for my coldness?' he asked, not entirely seriously.

'Oh, I wouldn't dream of such a thing,' she replied demurely, but his laugh warmed her as they began to climb the hill.

★ ★ ★

For a long time, Robert said nothing after Ellen Fairfax's voice had died away. He was trying to assimilate all the new ideas she had placed before him and readjust his assumptions.

The spot in which she had chosen to reveal the truth about her cousin's feelings for his sister — if, indeed, it *was* the truth — was eerie enough. They were high on the hillside, above the village, where the land levelled into a plateau dominated by a huge block of stone. An irregular cleft in its face formed a shallow cave, in which the breeze whispered.

While she had been speaking, Ellen had allowed her son to run about in the long grass, but she had not taken her eyes off him for more than a second and had once called him back when he had ventured too close to the Druid Stone, as if she were half-afraid it might have some sinister magical powers.

'But are you sure your cousin did not twist the truth?' Robert began abruptly.

She stopped him with a single direct look. 'I know Philip,' she said. 'He's not a man who wears his heart on his sleeve. But if you had heard him last night, you would not doubt him. Better yet, go and talk to him yourself.'

'I intend to.'

It was not that he thought she was lying. He was convinced that she believed her cousin. But Robert could not quite rid himself of a niggle of doubt that she might have been deceived by a clever liar. After all, did not all seducers rely on their ability to manipulate others and convince them that black was white?

Even assuming Philip Longridge had been telling her the truth, Robert would have wanted to talk to him in person. He needed to know what steps the other man had taken to trace Polly and her mother. Perhaps he had useful information that might enable him to find his family all the more quickly.

Not that Robert was looking forward to encountering the other man again. If Ellen Fairfax was right, he owed Philip Longridge an apology for the manner in which he had intruded in his home and accosted him in front of his guests.

Ellen smiled when he hinted at this to her. 'Oh, don't worry about Philip. His bark is much worse than his bite. Indeed, I sometimes think he only adopts that abrupt manner because he has such a soft heart and is afraid of being taken advantage of.'

Robert could not say that any of his observations bore out her statement; but, aware that he didn't really know the new squire, he remained silent on the subject. Instead he turned the conversation to the practicalities of finding his family.

'I'm afraid Philip didn't tell me much last night about his investigations,' Ellen said, 'except that he is pretty certain your mother and sister boarded the London coach. But he hasn't been able to ascertain whether they went all the way there or disembarked in some provincial town, or changed to another coach. But surely you must have a much better idea than Philip about whom your family might turn to in a crisis?'

Robert wished he shared her confidence. He felt as if he had been away from his family for far too long. He did not know enough about how they had lived and whom they had corresponded with while he was away.

'It would be so much easier if they had left some clue behind — ' he began, but was cut short by a sharp cry from his companion.

'Oh, of course!' she exclaimed. 'There are a number of locked trunks in the attic of my house — I believe Philip had your mother's former maid pack everything up ready, in case Mrs Lester or her daughter sent for their things. But they never have.'

Ellen Fairfax stopped, as if sensing the pang that cut through him at her last words. Was his family really so afraid of being traced? Or were they unable to send for their trunks, through illness or poverty or homelessness?

A gentle hand touched Robert's arm and a thrill darted through him.

'Perhaps things are not as bad as they

appear,' Ellen Fairfax suggested, those steady dove-grey eyes fixed on his.

'Perhaps,' he agreed.

It was a relief to be on good terms with her again, he realised. The thought that she was the beneficiary, perhaps even the inadvertent cause of his family's expulsion from the steward's house, had cast a shadow over his mind.

After her kindness to him on the night of his return, he had not wanted to believe she could be Philip Longridge's mistress rather than his cousin, as some of the villagers maintained. But that was nothing compared with what he had felt when she had apparently confirmed all the rumours by acting as if she were the mistress of the Grange and siding with the new squire.

It was the unselfconscious way that she spoke about her cousin that had set his mind at rest. He even felt ashamed of his suspicions about her character when he thought about the traces of emotion she had shown in the few brief references she had made to her husband.

'We really must be going,' Ellen Fairfax broke the silence. 'The wind is growing chill and I don't want Jemmy catching a cold.'

'Of course. You're going back home?'

'Yes.'

Robert made a sudden decision. 'If you have no objection, I'll escort you there and then go on to the Grange, in the hopes of finding Mr Longridge at home.'

'He might not be there at this hour of day,' Ellen warned him.

'No, I know. But I need to take as much exercise as I can, to build up my strength.'

'Are you not tired from making the journey twice last night?' she asked. 'I would hate it if you should get another bout of fever.'

Clearly she had spoken on impulse, because she reddened the instant she realised how her words might have sounded to an outsider.

'Oh, don't worry about me. One of the villagers agreed to take me to and from the Grange in his cart last night.'

It had been a shaky, jolting journey, uphill and down, but Robert felt it would have been ungrateful to complain, since it had spared him the need to wait until morning.

'If the squire is not at home, perhaps I could drop in at the steward's house on my way back and take a look at my mother's trunks?' he suggested tentatively.

'Of course you would be welcome,' she replied, though Robert wondered from the look in her eye whether she didn't experience a flutter of unease in case some gossip were to catch him calling upon her again.

They set off at a leisurely pace. Along the way, Robert told her that he had already taken the first step he could think of to find his family, by sending an advertisement to a number of prominent newspapers in London and Nottingham in the hopes that his family or somebody who knew them might see it.

The walk passed more quickly than Robert had expected. They danced delicately around their experiences of military life and found they had a great deal in common, though neither was willing just yet to talk about their experiences of the war in America.

Now and then they were forced to break off their conversation so Ellen could attend to her son or answer his questions. Robert found himself joining in, entertaining the little boy by quacking like a duck or neighing like a horse. When Jemmy's legs tired, his mother seated him astride her hip, his chubby little hands gripping her black cloak.

They had almost reached the steward's house when it happened. As they approached a bend in the road, they heard a woman's cry of alarm.

'Don't leave me!'

Another, softer voice responded with something Robert didn't catch. A second later a dishevelled, white-faced figure darted round the bend in the road. At the last second, she stumbled to a standstill and cast another look back over her shoulder, before she resumed her flight towards Ellen.

'Thank goodness you're here, Mrs Fairfax,' the young lady panted. 'Please help me. I don't know what to do.'

7

'Miss D'Arcy, whatever is the matter?'

The girl was too incoherent to answer Ellen Fairfax's question. Instead she grabbed the young widow by the sleeve and dragged her onward.

Robert put all his effort into propelling himself forward as quickly as he could in order to keep up. He was not sure what scene of disaster he expected to witness — an overturned coach at very least. So it was something of an anticlimax to find the rather grand lady he remembered intervening on Mr Longridge's behalf at the Grange seated on a stile and looking distinctly pale.

As he came closer, he noticed that her hat had been knocked askew and bent out of shape, while a thick smear of mud coated one side of her military-style riding habit.

At breakfast that morning, Robert's landlady had informed him of a rumour that Mr Longridge's sister Mrs Hume had just arrived at the Grange with her husband and his ward. Now as he looked closer, Robert thought he detected a family resemblance, particularly about the nose. Ellen Fairfax's next words confirmed his surmise.

'Caroline, what have you done to yourself?'

She broke free of Miss D'Arcy's convulsive grip and hurried towards her cousin.

'You make it sound as if I had done it on purpose,' the older woman retorted. It was only after she had spoken that she noticed Robert and flushed fiercely.

'No, no, of course I didn't mean that,' Ellen replied soothingly. 'What happened?'

Both Mrs Hume and Miss D'Arcy began to tell the story at the same time. From what Robert could gather, they had gone for a morning stroll, but had been frightened by a herd of cows in the meadow they had been crossing. Miss D'Arcy, being the younger and more nimble of the two, had negotiated the stile safely. Caroline Hume, in her agitation, had been less fortunate or more clumsy and so had taken a tumble, twisting her ankle so badly that she had been unable to take a single step further.

While this explanation had been taking place, Ellen had thrust Jemmy into the arms of a startled Miss D'Arcy and crouched beside her cousin. Robert too had lowered himself gingerly to the ground.

His first impulse had been to offer to carry the injured lady back to the Grange, or at least as far as the steward's cottage. It was only as he hobbled forward that he remembered why that was no longer possible.

'Please allow me to take a look,' he said.

In spite of the circumstances, Robert felt a frisson run through him as his arm brushed against Ellen Fairfax's. In an attempt to subdue his feelings, he probed Caroline Hume's ankle. Her protests at the unseemliness of this situation were cut short by a gasp of pain.

'I don't think anything is broken,' Robert said. 'Perhaps if it was bandaged up, it might be possible for you to put a little weight on it.'

He was already untying his cravat to fashion it into an improvised bandage. Meanwhile, a vigorous debate broke out about what they should do next.

'I would lend Mrs Hume my crutches,' Robert suggested, 'but I fear they are too long to be of any use.'

'Maybe I could run back to the Grange?' Amelia D'Arcy offered. 'I could order a carriage to come and collect Mrs Hume, and — '

'No, no, that will take far too long. I shall catch my death of cold, sitting in this damp spot,' Caroline Hume interrupted.

'Perhaps if Miss D'Arcy helped me to support you, Caroline, you could hobble back as far as my house,' Ellen Fairfax said. 'Mr Lester could go on ahead and warn Maggie that we are coming.'

Robert swallowed a bitter lump of impotence. Even a delicate girl like Miss D'Arcy was of more use in this situation than a poor cripple like himself. But this was not the right time to indulge in self-pity. Since Ellen's plan was the one that met the least opposition from the other ladies, he set out at once for the cottage.

The distance had never seemed so great before. Even when he had reached his destination, it felt like an intolerably long time before Maggie answered the door. But as soon as she had grasped what he was telling her, she was ready to go and relieve her mistress or Miss D'Arcy of their burden.

'There's a fire in the parlour to warm yourself.' Maggie tossed the words over her shoulder as she bustled away, still fiddling with the ribbons of her cloak.

But Robert could not bring himself

to loiter in the house that had once been his home, while the women toiled. He shook his head.

'Tell Mrs Fairfax I'm going to the Grange to send someone for the doctor and see if I can borrow a carriage for the ladies,' he said.

The shortest route lay, he judged, across the grounds of the Grange, particularly if he made straight for the stable-yard and avoided the house altogether. At present there was far too much on his mind. He didn't need the added complication of deciding how to approach the new squire.

Evidently Fate was not to be cheated in this way. As Robert entered the stable-yard, he found Philip Longridge dismounting from his horse after his morning ride. He turned his head and frowned at the sound of Robert's halting steps.

Robert set his jaw. This was no time to shrink back through embarrassment. 'I'm sorry for arriving like this, sir, but there's been an accident,' he panted.

He explained the situation as succinctly as he could. Philip Longridge's expression darkened, but he took charge at once, ordering one groom to set out for Mansfield for the doctor and another to hitch some horses to the chaise in order to convey the invalid back to the Grange.

While he was busy, Robert slipped away. He was anxious to return to the steward's house to make sure Ellen Fairfax and the others had reached it without any further mishap. But he could feel he was flagging. He was not used to taking so much exercise anymore.

'Mr Lester, wait!'

The cry made Robert whip his head round. Philip Longridge was hurrying after him on foot. Robert barely checked his impatience. It would have been rude to press on now and either way, it was impossible for him to outrun the other man.

'I want to apologise to you for the welcome you received at the Grange last night . . . ' Philip Longridge began, to Robert's astonishment.

'No, really, sir, there's no need for that,' he stammered. 'I was the one at fault. Mrs Fairfax has explained the — ah — situation to me.'

He saw Philip Longridge redden and averted his gaze so he could pretend not to have seen the squire's embarrassment.

'Yes, well, perhaps we are equally to blame for starting off on the wrong foot,' Philip Longridge said, somewhat stiffly. 'I trust we can behave in a more civilised manner in the future.'

'Agreed.'

'Good. Now let's go and see what my precious sister has done to herself this time.'

* * *

'You look exhausted, Mrs Fairfax.'

Ellen glanced up, startled by Robert Lester's voice so close beside her.

Hitherto all the fuss had centred on

127

Caroline. She had come close to fainting with pain more than once on their halting way back to the cottage. Amelia D'Arcy had done her best to support her guardian's wife, but she was only a slip of a girl and had been unspeakably grateful when Maggie had arrived to take her place.

It had been a relief to Ellen to be able to entrust Jemmy to the young heiress. He had been stumbling alongside her, clinging to her petticoats, and Ellen had found her attention torn between her responsibilities towards her son and her injured cousin.

She had indeed been exhausted, physically and emotionally, by the time she and Maggie had eased Caroline onto the couch, with her foot elevated. But there had been so much to do, to make Caroline comfortable, console Amelia and reassure Jemmy that Ellen had not had a chance to indulge in the luxury of sitting down.

Then Robert Lester and Philip had arrived, making the little house fuller than Ellen suspected it had been for a good long time.

The chaise had arrived soon afterwards, but Philip insisted that Caroline could not be moved until the surgeon had given his pronouncement and bandaged her foot properly, a process which was currently taking place.

'Oh, it's nothing,' Ellen replied to Robert Lester. 'Just the events of the day catching up with me.'

But she flushed under his grave look. It was a long time since any man had shown so much concern for her well-being. There was no opportunity for Robert to press his point, however, since the doctor had begun to pack his bag, while issuing instructions about Caroline's care.

Once he was ready to depart, the whole party trooped outside, Philip carrying his sister and Amelia sticking close by his side in her anxiety. So when Philip had deposited Caroline inside the chaise, he had no option but to hand Amelia in too, an action which made Caroline beam with triumph. Then her eye alighted upon Ellen and Robert Lester, who was still standing by her side.

'Oh, oh, before we go, might I have a word with you, Ellen?' she called out.

'Certainly.'

Ellen wove past Philip to the carriage door, imagining that her cousin intended to thank her. Instead Caroline grabbed her sleeve with both hands.

'A word to the wise,' she said in a hasty whisper. 'Beware of fortune-hunters. I'm sure you know what I mean.'

She gave Robert Lester such a significant look that Ellen wanted to laugh out loud. She lived in such a quiet, humble way, it was ludicrous to suggest that she might become prey to an unscrupulous man as, say, Amelia D'Arcy might. And yet, Ellen under-stood exactly what Caroline was hinting at.

'Don't worry, Caro,' she said. 'Even if

I were not capable of taking care of myself, I have Maggie to protect me.'

She drew back before her cousin could utter another word. In any case, Caroline had something else to concern her now.

'Are you not coming with us, Philip?' she called out as the carriage door was shut.

'No, I've business to discuss with Mr Lester,' Philip replied. 'I've ordered the chaise to return for us later. I intend to convey Mr Lester back to his lodgings by and by, so don't expect me for a while.'

And with that Caroline was forced to be content.

* * *

Ellen tilted her head to one side and surveyed her handiwork dubiously. She had never had a garden before and though she had asked Philip's gardener for advice, she was not at all sure she had planted her beans at the correct depth or the right distance from each other. Even so, she had found her experiment strangely satisfying.

Caroline, naturally, had disapproved of her decision to plant her own kitchen garden, rather than persuading Maggie or a casual labourer to lay out a flower garden for her — but then, Caroline had a wealthy husband and could afford to pay someone to look after both kinds of garden within the grounds of her home.

There would be a price to pay for her enjoyable afternoon, Ellen thought ruefully as she glanced at the other end of the vegetable bed. Jemmy was playing happily in the damp, soft earth, allowing the sand to trickle through his splayed fingers, gouging holes in the ground with a broken twig and calling excitedly for her to admire any strange creatures he disturbed.

It was wholly inevitable that his gown had suffered, and even more inevitable that Maggie would grumble when presented with the grubby garment to wash. Even if Ellen had offered to help with the laundry, Maggie was far too proud to accept.

'It's no job for a lady,' she had retorted on a previous occasion when Ellen had made the suggestion. 'It's bad enough you do as much as you do. There's no call for you to debase yourself any further.'

Ellen sighed and returned to her digging. It was more than two weeks since her life had returned to its usual routine after those few flurried days of activity. So why was it that she still felt unsettled?

After the chaise containing Caroline and Amelia had left, Ellen had invited Philip and Robert Lester back into the house, to await the return of the carriage. It had been quite obvious to her that her former patient was exhausted from his exertions and needed to sit down.

Both men had accepted her invitation and after a little initial stiffness, Philip had told Robert what little he had been able to glean about the movements of Mrs Lester and her daughter since their departure.

'As far as I can tell, they are in London, but it's such a vast place, it's hard to decide where to begin looking.'

'Perhaps it will not be as difficult to find them as you think,' Robert replied, before telling Philip about the advertisement.

But Philip looked no more cheerful than before.

'I hope you're right,' he said, 'but I fear Mrs Lester may suspect it is simply a ruse, intended to flush them out into the open.'

Robert had looked so dejected by this possibility that Ellen hastily changed the subject to what else might be done to find the fugitives.

'You've no idea, I suppose, what became of Jane, the servant who used to work for my mother?' Robert asked, aiming the question chiefly at Philip.

'As a matter of fact I do,' the other man replied. 'I gave her a job at the

Grange, since she seemed a capable girl. But if she does know where her former mistress went, she has been warned not to say anything to me. Which doesn't mean that she might not have something to tell *you*.'

The eyes of the two men locked.

'When do you suppose would be a good time to speak to her?' Robert asked.

Philip frowned. 'If I'm not mistaken, she asked me a few days ago for leave to go home and nurse her sick mother. I believe she has a number of younger siblings, so I told her not to hurry back before her mother had recovered fully.'

'Oh,' Robert said. 'Well, perhaps I can call on her at home. Her family comes from Papplewick, or one of those villages on the Nottingham turnpike, don't they?'

But Philip shook his head.

'I'm sorry, I've no idea. Perhaps one of the other servants would know.'

While he was at the steward's house, Robert had also had a cursory hunt through the trunks of possessions his family had left behind, but found little to aid his search, apart from the addresses of some family friends on old letters.

'I doubt they know anything, but it's worth turning every stone.' He sighed. 'I suppose there is nothing else for it. I shall have to go to visit them in person to assure them I really am alive.'

Philip offered to accompany him, but Robert thought it better to go on his own, in case his mother or sister caught sight of the wrong man and took flight once more. He did, however, reluctantly accept a small loan from the squire to pay for his expenses. He had squeezed Ellen's hand in parting and thanked her for her help, and she had not seen or heard anything from him since.

Now and then Jemmy asked in his garbled fashion, 'Misty Lesty tum back?' because during that last meeting the former soldier had endeared himself still further to the little boy by bouncing him on his knee and feeding him cake crumbs whenever he thought Ellen wasn't watching.

But Ellen had never been able to give Jemmy a satisfactory answer. Would Robert Lester come back? If his family had settled somewhere else, would he not stay with them? The best she could hope for was that he might write to her or to Philip to report his progress. And if Miss Lester had taken a dislike to Philip and persisted in rejecting him, would it not be better for them to stay as far away from Nottinghamshire as possible?

'Well, Jemmy,' Ellen said now, sitting back on her heels to stretch out her back and ease her hunched shoulders, 'I think that might be enough work for one day, don't you think?'

As a reply, Jemmy deposited two handfuls of soil on top of his head so it trickled down his face and the nape of his neck.

'Jemmy, no! Maggie will be so cross with both of us for letting you get so dirty.'

137

But Jemmy did not seem the slightest bit put out by this protest, though he squirmed when his mother tried to brush him down and make him look halfway presentable.

It was while she was in the midst of this that Ellen's ear caught an unusual sound. Carts and carriages rarely passed this way. She was even more surprised when she raised her head and found a gentleman's coach approaching instead of the farm cart she had anticipated.

It must be visitors looking for the Grange who had inexplicably missed the grand front gates, Ellen thought as she scrambled upright, brushing at her gown and apron in a vain attempt to rid them of earth and smooth out the creases.

And then her heart jolted. The carriage had stopped at her gate. The livery of the servant who descended from the coach, the coat of arms on its door — no, it couldn't be.

But she couldn't mistake the elderly

man in the powdered bagwig who descended from the coach. It was undoubtedly her father-in-law and Jemmy's paternal grandfather.

8

Ellen's first instinct was to snatch Jemmy up. She was conscious that she had never appeared less to her advantage than now, grubby from her afternoon's work and with her son in a similarly filthy condition — the picture of neglect, if you overlooked his sturdy limbs, round cheeks and the mischievous glint in his eyes.

'My good woman . . . ' Mr Fairfax began in the patronising tone he reserved for the lower orders. Then he took a closer look at Ellen and checked himself. 'Good Lord, it's much worse than I thought.'

The palpable disgust with which he regarded her made Ellen raise her chin.

'How did you find me?'

Even as the words sprang to her lips, the solution came to Ellen. On the day after Caroline's accident, she had gone to the Grange to see how her cousin was faring and instead found herself the recipient of a long lecture about the dangers of trusting her reputation to an impoverished, one-legged fortune-hunter.

'Oh, come now, Caroline, I am hardly a great catch.'

Caroline stared at her coldly.

'*You* may not be,' she retorted, 'but Jemmy is the sole heir to a considerable fortune. Any man who inveigled himself into your good graces might assume it would be no difficult matter to gain control of that fortune while Jemmy is still a minor.'

'Mr Fairfax is still very much alive and looks after his finances himself.'

But Caroline dismissed this with a toss of the head. As always when confronted with an argument she did not want to address, she changed her grounds of attack.

'I don't know why you choose to live as you do, when you ought to be bringing up Jemmy to be a gentleman.

There is really no need for this. If you would only swallow your pride and apologise to Mr Fairfax . . . '

It was an argument Ellen had heard so many times, she had barely paid any attention to it. Now it seemed that her cousin had taken matters into her own hands and had decided to forge a reconciliation. No doubt she had the very best of intentions, but Caroline had no idea what manner of man she was dealing with.

Mr Fairfax did not deign to answer Ellen's question. Instead he threw a contemptuous glance at the modest sandstone house behind her, before his gaze returned to Jemmy. Having taken one look at his grandfather, the boy had clenched his arms tight around his mother's neck and buried his face on her shoulder.

Clearly Jemmy had not forgotten his grandfather, or the scenes that had occurred before that fateful morning when Ellen realised she had finally had enough and had packed her possessions and left with Jemmy and Maggie.

Ellen cleared her throat. 'Why are you here?'

'I hardly think it is appropriate to discuss such matters in front of the servants,' Mr Fairfax replied coldly.

Ellen swallowed hard. Every instinct told her not to let this man across the threshold of her sanctuary. But she knew there would be consequences if she tried to run indoors and slam the door in his face. Mr Fairfax was not used to being thwarted and would not let someone he considered to be puny and insignificant oppose his will or humiliate him in front of his servants.

And he was right about one thing. She could almost see the ears of his footman and coachman flapping while they pretended to be absorbed in examining their surroundings or tending to the horses.

Indoors Maggie at least would be within calling distance, Ellen told herself. Mustering as much dignity as she could, despite her dishevelled appearance, she picked her way along the path to the front door.

'You'd better come in, sir,' she said, though she could not prevent the last word from sounding like an insult.

The elderly man sniffed disapprovingly, but nonetheless he followed her into the narrow hallway. There she handed Jemmy over to Maggie, with instructions to make him look presentable.

Ellen removed her apron, but she resisted the urge to excuse herself to go and wash her hands and change her shoes and gown. She wanted to get this interview over and done with as quickly as possible and she had no intention of giving Mr Fairfax the opportunity to wander, unattended, about her parlour, finding yet more faults in her as the guardian of her own son.

Mr Fairfax's expression as he glanced round the shabby parlour, with its small windows and scratched or threadbare furniture, told Ellen all she needed to know. There was a sort of triumph in his eyes, as if he thought that the humble way she lived was an indication that he had been right all along and she could not survive long on her own and would therefore be amenable to anything he offered her.

She had to clench her fists to control her temper when she saw the superior smirk twitching at the corners of his thin lips.

I won't ask him to explain himself again, she thought fiercely. *Let him do it in his own good time. Nor will I ask him to sit down.*

'Well,' he said stiffly, once he had taken everything in, 'as you may have surmised, I have come here to make a proposition to you. I am willing to settle a considerable sum of money upon you for life, so you can live a great deal more comfortably than you do at present.'

But Ellen knew him too well from the months she had spent living under his roof after her return from America.

'Very generous of you, sir,' she

replied, 'but on what conditions?'

Mr Fairfax did not even blink.

'On the condition that you entrust the welfare and education of your son entirely to me and my wife.'

Ellen was struck dumb by the audacity of his demand. She had expected him to ask her to return to live with them as before. This was far, far worse than she had ever anticipated.

'You want me to give up my *son*?' she whispered.

He seemed not to pick up on her tone.

'Naturally you would be allowed to visit him from time to time,' he said as smoothly as if it was the most reasonable proposal in the world. 'But my wife and I feel that you would be a — disruptive influence upon the boy and — '

'No! I won't hear of it!'

Mr Fairfax seemed taken aback by the vehemence of her cry, but it did not shake his conviction.

'You must see that we are in a far better position to provide for young James than you are ever likely to be. The right education, the right connections, in time a suitable profession and wife . . . '

'He's not even three years old.'

But this protest only elicited a patronising smile.

'Surely the sooner a seedling is transplanted to fertile soil, the more it will flourish,' he replied. 'You cannot expect that cousin of yours to provide for the boy. He'll get bored with your demands soon enough and I gather he is contemplating matrimony himself. With a family of his own, he is hardly likely to want James hanging round his neck like a millstone.'

'I have no intention of taking advantage of my cousin, or making demands of him, as you so charmingly phrase it.'

Mr Fairfax curled his lip contemptuously as he looked her up and down.

'I suppose you mean to get married

again,' he said, 'but trust me, living in this backwater, you won't meet many gentlemen willing and able to take responsibility for another man's child. Whereas if you hand over your son to us and accept the annuity I am offering you, you are far more likely to meet someone suitable . . . '

'I'd never marry a man who did not care for my son or who wished me to disown him as if he were illegitimate.'

A sudden image flashed before Ellen's eyes of Robert Lester bouncing Jemmy on his knee and feeding him illicit cake.

'There is no question of your disowning young James,' Mr Fairfax replied, as if explaining something to a simpleton. 'Merely of doing what is best for your son.'

'Maybe my notions of what is best for my son differ from yours.'

Mr Fairfax merely rolled his eyes at her words, evidently dismissing them as a romantic flight of fancy.

'And what about his education? Are

you going to let him grow up a little savage?'

'I am quite capable of teaching him to read and write when the time comes. And when he is a little older, there is a perfectly adequate grammar school in Mansfield and scholarships to Cambridge available to diligent . . . '

'Scholarships? Outrageous!' Mr Fairfax exploded without warning. 'I won't have my grandson brought up like — like a charity case. Do you realise what I am worth? Do you have any idea what that boy is heir to, unless you provoke me too far and I disinherit him?'

His roar seemed to shake the whole house. Ellen heard Jemmy begin to cry upstairs and she was not sure if it was in response to his grandfather's bellow or for some other reason. But for his sake, she had to cut this confrontation short, so she could go and comfort him.

'Mr Fairfax,' she said, controlling herself with an effort, 'we have discussed this matter over and over again.

The reason I left your house was because the constant struggles over my son's future were making him so unhappy. If you have nothing new to say to me, I would like you to leave.'

Mr Fairfax glared at her, his white, tufted eyebrows drawn together so they almost touched above his nose. She braced herself for another explosion.

'I shall give you one last opportunity to reconsider,' he said slowly, like a man pushed to the very limits of his patience. 'Will you accept my proposal or not?'

For a second, Ellen thought of all the things she would have liked to provide for her son, but could not afford. He would not even be able to buy himself a commission in his father's old regiment, unless one of James's fellow officers took an interest in him — assuming that any of James's closest friends survived the war.

But the alternative was unthinkable.

'You already have my answer, sir. I shall not change my mind.'

Mr Fairfax sniffed, but to Ellen's surprise, he strode stiffly past her to the outer door. She followed in a daze, hardly daring to believe that it was all over. That Mr Fairfax had given up. That she had won.

And then, on the doorstep, he swung round to face her again.

'Don't think for a second that this is over,' he said, 'or that I will allow my grandson to grow up in such — squalor.'

In spite of herself, Ellen flinched at the last word.

'Hardly squalor, sir,' she replied, keeping her voice low to stop it trembling. 'If you had cared to look, you would have found the house spotlessly clean. I assure you my son lacks for neither food nor clothing nor any of the other necessities of life.'

There was something so deeply unpleasant in the smile Mr Fairfax bestowed on her that Ellen shuddered.

'Well, we shall see if a court of law agrees with your assessment of the situation, shall we?' he replied. 'I doubt I shall have any difficulty in proving you an unfit mother and an inadequate guardian for the boy, since I gather you have been entertaining male callers before you are even out of second mourning.'

Ellen reeled at his words. She could not help herself. She knew how cruel and unjustified the allegation was. She also knew that as a woman, and a poor one too, she was highly unlikely to be able to obtain justice in a court of law against all the might of Mr Fairfax's wealth.

'Mrs Fairfax, what on earth is the matter? Are you unwell?'

The sound of that voice made Ellen look up sharply. She hadn't dared believe it was true, but there on the path, near the gate, stood Robert Lester.

Pleasure and relief welled up inside her at the sight of a sympathetic face. But almost instantly a little poisonous whisper flitted through her mind.

Would his arrival confirm in Mr Fairfax's mind that the rumours he had heard about her character were true? Would he use this unexpected visit against her to deprive her of her son?

She had to gather her wits. She was aware that Mr Fairfax was eyeing the newcomer dubiously and something about Robert Lester's expression and even his stance suggested that he did not entirely trust the older man and suspected that he might have had something to do with Ellen's apparent indisposition.

'No, I am not ill, thank you, sir,' she replied, more formally than she would have done if her father-in-law had not been present.

She saw Robert flinch barely perceptibly at her tone. Had she alienated him too?

'I can come back at some other time if it is not convenient for me to call at present,' Robert Lester offered.

'Oh, no, no, sir,' Mr Fairfax intervened. 'I should not dream of standing in your way. In any case, I was just leaving.'

And with one last triumphant look at Ellen, as if he had caught her in a misdeed, he hobbled away towards his waiting coach.

In a vain attempt to rectify matters, she was tempted to call him back, to offer him some excuse for Robert Lester's call. Even to beg Mr Fairfax to reconsider his threat to go to court. But in her heart of hearts, she knew her father-in-law was determined to think the worst of her and she was too proud to beg.

Ellen closed her eyes for a moment and heard the carriage door shut.

'Mrs Fairfax?' Robert Lester asked softly. 'Who was that?'

She opened her eyes and mustered a bitter smile.

'That's the man who is going to ruin my life,' she replied simply.

★ ★ ★

'That's outrageous.' Robert could not restrain his feelings any longer. 'On what grounds can he possibly claim you are an unfit mother?'

All his weariness after a long and fruitless journey was swept away by his indignation on Ellen Fairfax's behalf. He had questioned the wisdom of his impulsive decision to return to Mansfield in order to see her again and confide his troubles in her. Now he was glad he had come, because otherwise she might never have told him about this threat to her happiness.

She shrugged in answer to his question.

'He is rich. I am not. It's as simple as that,' she said. 'It doesn't help that both Jemmy and I were grubby from digging in the garden when Mr Fairfax arrived.'

But Robert shook his head. The way she avoided meeting his eye told him there was something she was keeping from him.

'Hardly grounds for claiming you are a harmful influence on Jemmy,' he said.

'What else did he say . . . oh.'

The truth dawned on him with blinding clarity. How else was a woman ever discredited by a vindictive man, except through casting aspersions on her chastity? And when he recalled Mr Fairfax's parting sneer, Robert found all the proof he needed to confirm his conjecture.

'He is determined to blacken your character, isn't he?' he said. Her instinctive flinch was answer enough. 'And I have made matters worse by arriving at precisely the wrong moment, when not only he, but his servants were able to witness it.'

'Oh, come now, it's not as if they caught us in a compromising situation,' Ellen blustered, flushing at the very thought.

But Robert was not convinced. He could see that she was afraid that something so innocent could be twisted by a malicious mind and used as a weapon against her.

Robert's thoughts whirled. He could

not allow Ellen to lose custody of her son. He had seen how passionately she loved Jemmy. He knew all the arguments against it — the slightness of their acquaintance, her obvious love for her dead husband, his lost leg and, most importantly, his current inability to maintain himself, much less his family and hers too — and yet, the words came impulsively to his lips.

'Well, if there is no other way to preserve your good name, will you marry me?'

9

For a moment, Ellen could do nothing but stare at the man in front of her. Her blood pounded in her ears. All sorts of unexpected emotions flooded through her. Had he really said what she thought he had said?

But as she stood there, frozen, words began to tumble from Robert's lips, trying to anticipate any objections she might have to such a sudden change of circumstances.

'Mr Lester,' she interrupted the flow as gently as possible, 'please don't think I'm ungrateful. I am flattered by your regard, but you must see how impossible this is . . . '

For a second, the idea that she might have said 'yes' flashed across her mind. No need to be on her own any more, in sole charge of Jemmy's welfare. Protected from the slanders of the world by this handsome, generous man, who reminded her of James in so many ways.

But wouldn't such an imprudent second match make Mr Fairfax even more determined to claim custody of Jemmy? And would it be fair to accept Robert Lester's offer when her feelings for her dead husband were still so strong?

Robert gave her a wry smile.

'No, I suppose you're right,' he said heavily. 'I have nothing to offer you — no position in life, no home, not even a full complement of limbs . . . '

Ellen could not repress a cry at this.

'Don't ever think that the loss of your leg could lower you in my esteem,' she said, laying her hand upon his arm. 'But the circumstances, this situation . . . '

She faltered, unable to find the right words. Just gazing into Robert's eyes was overwhelming. Her hand was still resting on his arm and a current seemed to pulse between them, as if somehow, indefinably, they had become part of the same entity.

'No, I understand,' he said at last, swallowing hard as he averted his face to break their gaze. 'I am in no position to offer you any security, even assuming that . . . and of course you are still in mourning for your husband.'

'Yes,' Ellen agreed, but the word trailed away uncertainly.

Because she realised belatedly that it wasn't true. It would have been quite within the bounds of propriety for her to resume wearing colours now, only there had never seemed any pressing need to do so, not while the black gowns were still presentable enough not to need replacing.

A memory broke the surface of her mind.

'If I should die . . . ' James had begun, while she stuck her fingers in her ears and declared she would not even contemplate such a thing.

But he had taken both her hands, held them tight, forced her to look up at him.

'If I should die, Ellen, you must not mourn me forever. You must promise me that. You are still young and if you waste the rest of your life pining, I will not rest in peace.'

Ellen shook herself. It was not like her to dwell on sorrows that could not be changed. She looked up at Robert Lester.

'I'm sorry. I've been so self-absorbed. I haven't even asked you how your quest went.'

Robert mustered a smile.

'No luck, I'm afraid,' he said. 'I've talked to a lot of people, renewed my acquaintance with various old family friends and relatives, but none of them seem to have seen or heard anything of my mother or Polly since my presumed death.'

Ellen could see that although he was making light of it, he had found the whole process something of an ordeal, both physically and mentally.

'What about Jane? That *was* the name of your mother's servant, wasn't it? Did you manage to speak to her?'

Again he gave her a pained smile.

'Just my luck,' he said. 'By the time I reached her parents' cottage, I discovered she had left at dawn that same morning to return to work at the Grange. I must have missed her by just a few hours. Since I was almost halfway to Nottingham, it didn't seem worthwhile retracing my steps when I knew there was a good chance I would return here anyway, whatever the outcome of my search. But I don't suppose she knows anything useful anyway.'

'You don't know that for certain. Is there no other avenue you could explore as well?' Ellen urged. 'Your family can't have vanished off the face of the earth.'

'That's what I thought, but I am beginning to change my mind,' Robert replied.

His expression gave Ellen a pang. She had never seen him look so defeated before.

'Do you have any plans for the

future?' she asked, half-afraid of uttering the words because she did not want to upset him.

He shook his head.

'I've thought and thought of nothing else, but I can't see my way forward,' he said. 'I know I ought to find myself some employment, but I am not sure that I will be able to settle while this uncertainty still hovers over my head.'

Her heart went out to him.

'I know how you feel,' she said. 'When James was missing . . . '

She couldn't go on.

'How long is it since your husband died?'

It took Ellen a second to register Robert's question and to nerve herself to reply.

'A little more than a year. He was involved in the rearguard action on the Princeton to Trenton road, just after Christmas in 1776. I don't know much more than that.'

She forced herself to stop before she made herself cry. It was strange that her feelings could suddenly feel so raw again. She had thought she had cried enough to last a lifetime. But every now and then, something would remind her.

She had not dared cry at first, when she heard that James's regiment had been involved in a series of counter-attacks. She had been left behind in New York with Jemmy and Maggie when the British Army had gone in pursuit of Washington's rebels as they retreated from White Plains, across New Jersey and into Delaware.

From the start, news had been sketchy and letters infrequent. And then Washington had re-crossed the ice-filled Delaware River, in the teeth of the most ferocious snowstorm of the winter, and wreaked havoc on the lowered guard of the British Army's Hessian allies at Trenton.

There had been confusion and rumour in New York. Lt-Gen Lord Cornwallis had cancelled his plans to return to England to visit his ailing wife. There was talk of a minor skirmish on the road and of the Americans looting Princeton before retreating to Morristown, to belatedly take up winter quarters. Talk of a number of British soldiers — some said 200, others more or less — being captured when they tried to take a stand, some of them from James's regiment.

For days, Ellen did not sleep. She questioned anyone and everyone for news, strained her eyes for familiar faces on the streets of New York, paced the floor of her lodgings till the day's post had arrived. Nothing. Not a word from her husband.

She was tempted to cross over to New Jersey and seek news in person at Amboy or New Brunswick, the two remaining British outposts. Maggie might not have succeeded in talking her out of such a rash expedition if it had not been for the baby. Jemmy was scarcely eighteen months old, far too young to brave the winter weather, and Ellen could not have left him behind, unless Maggie agreed to stay with him.

'No, Mrs Fairfax, my place is with you. I wouldn't trust anyone else in these foreign parts to keep an eye on you. I know how wilful you can be. You'd risk your neck and then what would become of the poor little orphan?'

'You would take care of him,' Ellen had replied and Maggie smiled grimly because they both knew that it was true. If anything were to happen to Ellen, Maggie would bring up Jemmy as if he were her own — if Mr Fairfax would permit it.

For a long time Ellen had clung to the hope that James was among those captured. If he was still alive, there was a chance that he might be exchanged for American prisoners and would return safe and well and capable of fighting another day.

She wrote letter after letter, to anyone she could think of — to her husband's senior officers; to his fellow captains and the subalterns who had served under him; to the American officers in charge of the prisoners, in the hope that someone somewhere would know something.

And then at last came the meeting she had never wanted to occur.

'I saw him fall. He died a hero's death, leading his men. It was quick, clean and without pain.'

But Ellen had been an officer's daughter and an officer's wife long enough to know that might well have been a kindly lie. Oh, James was undoubtedly dead. The few effects the officer returned to her proved that. But it was possible his death had been neither quick nor clean nor painless. Nevertheless that was the myth she would perpetuate when Jemmy was old enough to ask how he had lost his papa.

She did not tell Robert Lester everything, but it was a relief nonetheless to relive some of that dark time with someone who knew better than most about the confusion and ugliness of war.

He did not say much, but she could

not mistake his sympathy. There were none of the fatuous or sanctimonious comments that she had had to endure from those who meant well, but understood nothing about the reality of the situation.

A momentary silence descended over the parlour. The sombre mood was broken, however, by the sound of running steps. The handle of the door rattled as small, inexpert fingers reached up to grasp it and, more by accident than design, Jemmy half-tumbled into the room with the momentum of the opening door.

From a distance, Ellen could hear Maggie's scolding voice, but this was drowned out when Jemmy looked up at his mother's visitor, recognised him and, with a beam of delight, flung both arms around Robert's one sound leg.

'Misty Lesty!' he declared and then began to babble so rapidly and unintelligibly that even Ellen had difficulty in deciphering what he intended to say.

Robert's face cleared at the sight of the little boy. He swung him up onto his knee and began to grope in the pockets of his shabby red coat.

'I have something for you,' he said, producing a little wooden horse with a flourish.

And so it was that ten minutes later, when Philip called in on his cousin on his way home, he discovered Robert Lester crouched on the hearthrug with Jemmy, playing with the new toy as well as half a dozen somewhat battered toy soldiers and an improvised fort built of wooden blocks.

Ellen was sitting nearby, pretending to darn boy-sized stockings, but she could not help stealing the occasional glance at the comical scene at her feet.

Robert scrambled up at the sight of the newcomer. Ellen noticed there was still an element of reserve between the two men, but this melted away when Philip came up with an unexpected proposal.

'I've been thinking things over

during the past weeks and I wondered if you would like to work for me, Lester? I could do with someone to help me with my correspondence and to ride out to the outlying farms to see what work needs to be done. From what I can make out, my uncle let business matters slip somewhat in the last year or two of his life, partly because he refused to employ another steward in your father's place, even though his own health was beginning to fail.'

Robert did not reply immediately. A frown had creased his brow and he bounced Jemmy distractedly on his knee.

'I won't deny it is a tempting proposition,' he said, stealing a glance at Ellen, who found herself blushing in spite of herself. 'And if I knew my mother and sister were safe and well provided for, I would not hesitate to accept. But . . . '

'Yes, yes, of course. I understand. You needn't give me a definitive answer yet.

I can manage for a while longer on my own.'

And with that, the matter was dropped for the time being.

⋆   ⋆   ⋆

Robert was bone-weary by the time he arrived in Blidworth. He had left the cottage at the same time as Philip, not only to protect Ellen's name, but also so he could inform the other man of Mr Fairfax's threat to claim custody of his grandson.

Philip had been suitably indignant and alarmed on his cousin's behalf and promised to do all he could to prevent such an outcome.

'I'll talk to Mr Fairfax myself and see if I can't persuade him to change his mind,' he said. 'If that fails, Ellen shall have the best legal advice I can afford.'

It was entirely typical of Ellen that she had not mentioned her own troubles to her cousin, Robert thought, as he made his way towards the village.

Instead she had concentrated on what might be done to find Robert's family. He felt a little better now, as if he had paid some of the debt of gratitude he owed her.

All the time he had been away, he had been unable to stop thinking about her. When he had seen her looking so vulnerable as she confronted her father-in-law, all Robert had wanted to do was fling himself into the breach and defend her in any way he could — which only served to make his powerlessness more galling.

And then of course there was the ghost of her dead husband. It was clear to him she would never cease to love James Fairfax. How could he possibly compete? Yet he could not bear to stay away from her for long. It made Philip Longridge's offer of employment almost irresistible. And yet, if Ellen would never be able to return his feelings, would he simply drive himself mad, trying to be no more than a friend to her?

He was greeted at the inn like a long-lost son. Before long, he found himself seated by the cheering fire — the evenings still being chill — while he awaited his supper.

'You've a visitor.'

The landlord's announcement made him jump.

'For me?' How had anyone heard about his return so soon? 'Who is it?'

He was rising from his seat when he spotted a familiar figure, half-hidden behind the landlord. A young woman with work-worn hands and a homespun cloak.

'Jane?'

'Mr Longridge said he'd seen you at the cottage,' she replied, rumpling her apron nervously. 'I think he meant it as a hint I ought to come and talk to you.'

She was staring at him as if she had never seen him before and Robert had to remind himself that until a few weeks ago, she, like everyone else in this neighbourhood, had thought he was dead.

'I can't believe it's really you, sir,' she added.

'It's good to be back,' Robert said, wishing once more that he had written a second letter to his mother after recovering from his amputation. But he hadn't wanted her to incur the expense of the postage. 'Won't you sit down?'

Jane hesitated, then perched on the edge of the settle opposite him.

'I'm sure you must have guessed why I'm anxious to speak to you,' Robert went on, as soon as he had lowered himself into his seat and propped his crutches against the armrest. 'Do you have any idea where my mother and sister went after they left the cottage? Or anything at all about the events that led to their departure?'

But Jane shook her head.

'I'm not sure there's much I can tell you that'd be useful,' she said warily. 'Mrs Lester didn't confide in me and neither did Miss Lester and I don't listen at doors.'

'No, no, of course not.'

'All I know is that a week or two before they made their flit, Miss Lester came home from the village looking as if she'd been crying along the way and she and Mrs Lester were shut away in her bedroom for hours afterwards, talking.'

'Oh.' Robert felt disappointment wash over him. For the first time, he realised how much he had been hoping that Jane might know something. Now that avenue was closed, he had no idea what to do next.

But Jane was not done yet.

'I knew they were planning something after that,' she said, furrowing her brow. 'They sent me out on a lot of errands, as if they didn't want me about the house as much as usual. And I do know they settled all their bills, because Mr Longridge asked about it afterwards. But I never expected them to go like they did.'

'Surely they didn't just leave you without an explanation?' Robert urged. It seemed so out of character for his mother to behave in such a manner.

'No, sir, they didn't,' she confirmed. 'The day before it happened, I was getting the supper ready when I heard Miss Lester slam the door and dash up the stairs in a tearing hurry. The mistress went up to speak to her and then she came into the kitchen to talk to me.'

Jane rubbed her forehead as if the strain of remembering was making it ache.

'She hummed and ha-ed for a while and then told me she and the young mistress were obliged to go away very suddenly and they'd decided they'd better leave me behind because my family's here. She said she wasn't displeased with my work, I wasn't to think that, and she gave me a letter of recommendation so I'd be able to find another place and a month's wages in lieu of notice on condition that I wouldn't breathe a word to anyone, not even the squire, about anything I'd seen or heard — even though I didn't *know* anything. But she'd always been a good mistress, so I promised I'd keep quiet.'

So Philip Longridge had been right in thinking Jane had been sworn to silence, Robert thought. But it still didn't help him much.

'She asked me to deliver a letter to the Grange, but not till late the following morning, after they'd gone, and to lock up the cottage and take the key back to the squire,' Jane continued. 'They went that same night — to Mansfield, I suppose, to catch the early coach and I did as I was told. Though it was eerie, spending the whole night in that cottage on my own. I swear I didn't sleep a wink.'

'How did the squire react when you took him the letter?' Robert asked.

Was there anything suspicious in the fact that Philip Longridge had neglected to tell him about this?

'He ripped it open there and then in front of me and when he'd read it, he rang the bell and flitted about the room, as if he'd forgotten I was there.

And then suddenly he turned on me and began asking me questions I couldn't answer, like where they'd gone and when, but he hardly had the patience to listen to my replies and when someone answered the bell, he asked to have his horse saddled instantly. Oh, and then, as if he'd only just thought of it, he asked me if I was in need of a new place and promised he'd find me one if I proved myself trustworthy.'

By which he probably meant if she proved she could hold her tongue and not gossip about what she had witnessed, Robert thought.

'And that's all, is it? You're sure there's nothing else you've forgotten to tell me?'

Again Jane shook her head.

'No. Oh, except — '

'Except what?'

'Well, I don't know if it means anything, but I think it was on the morning after Miss Lester's first upset that the mistress sent me to Mansfield to put a letter in the post.'

'A letter?' Robert echoed. 'I don't suppose you remember the address or anything else about it?'

'No, but I know there was a letter arrived from Derby maybe a week later because the mistress didn't have the right change for the postman and Miss Lester had to pay for it out of her purse.'

'Derby,' Robert repeated thoughtfully. 'You're sure it was Derby?'

What acquaintances did his mother have in Derby? He couldn't think of anyone and yet it felt significant.

'Oh, yes, sir, I'm quite sure. It isn't as if vast numbers of letters ever came there.'

Robert thanked her distractedly, but long after she had gone, he found himself brooding on the problem. Derby was at least a good starting point for his search and thankfully it was not as large a town as Nottingham. But he was not sure how easy it would be to find any trace of his family without any better clue. After all, he had no absolute confirmation that that was where his mother and sister had gone.

He was still turning the problem over in his mind the following morning at breakfast when a letter arrived for him. Robert could not prevent excitement from rising inside him. Surely the only way anyone could have known to write to him at this address was if they had seen the advertisement he had placed in the newspaper?

It was with a crushing sense of disappointment that Robert realised that the handwriting on the covering sheet did not belong to his mother or his sister. Indeed, he was not sure that he recognised it at all.

Steeling himself, in case it proved a hoax or an attempt to extort money, he broke the seal and unfolded the sheet.

* * *

'Mr Lester!'

It was the second time Ellen had

called his name, he having apparently not heard her first cry. She had emerged on her doorstep just in time to see him limping past the cottage. Now she broke into a run to catch up with him.

He turned and Ellen half-flinched from his grim expression.

'What on earth is the matter?' she gasped.

He let out a long breath, to try to ease his panting. He had been limping towards Mansfield at a faster pace than Ellen had ever seen him employ.

'I must get to the Swan,' he said. 'I've got to catch the Nottingham coach . . . '

Ellen shook her head as she closed both hands round his upper arm to halt his jagged progress.

'You're too late. The coach was due to leave half an hour ago,' she said. 'Even if it were delayed, I doubt you could get there in time.'

He limped forward two more paces, before he flagged, accepting the inevitability of her words. She could see that he had perhaps known his quest was impossible from the outset, but he had not wanted to admit it.

He uttered a moan and closed his eyes.

'The Sheffield to London coach passes through Mansfield tomorrow,' Ellen said, still in the dark as to what could have caused his sudden desperation to get away. 'That goes through Nottingham as well.'

Eyes still closed, he shook his head.

'By tomorrow, it may be too late,' he said and Ellen's heart contracted in sympathy as he opened his eyes. There was such a look of pain and sadness in his face.

'Too late for what?' she asked.

Robert took in another gulp of air. He was shaking in reaction to his recent exertions and he did not resist when she tugged him towards her cottage.

'Why don't you come inside and catch your breath and then you can tell me all about it,' Ellen suggested, because she could see he needed to rest.

'I received a letter,' he said, between gasps for breath as he began to hobble towards the house. 'It only arrived this morning, or else I would have set out earlier.'

'Bad news?' Ellen asked.

'Yes. It's from one of my mother's old friends in Derby. Mamma is very ill. She — the friend, I mean — had seen my advertisement and shown it to Polly, but Polly thought it must have been placed by someone who meant her harm — that's the phrase Mrs Knight uses in her letter — and she wouldn't reply to it, but Mrs Knight took it upon herself to write to me instead, because she thought it was only right that Polly's family should know where she is in this time of need and . . . '

He ran out of breath, but fortunately by this time Ellen had managed to get him inside the house. She opened the parlour door and guided him to the armchair.

'You're sure this letter is genuine?' Ellen asked. 'It couldn't be a mistake or a trick, could it?'

Again Robert shook his head.

'The details match. I think I even remember meeting Mrs Knight once, when I was a boy. They've been surviving by taking in sewing and Polly's been doing some copying for a local lawyer, but of course she can't work while Mamma is ill — oh God, what if she's dead and Polly's all alone?'

His stricken look touched Ellen's heart.

'She isn't all alone, even if the worst has happened,' she pointed out softly, taking his cold hand between her own and gazing into his face to impress her words upon him. 'This Mrs Knight sounds as if she would look after your sister whenever and however she could. And you will be there soon too.'

She waited till he responded to her with wry smile, before she got up and released his hand. She opened the lid of her writing desk and examined the nib

184

of her pen in case it needed mending. Then she extracted a fresh sheet of paper and opened the inkwell.

'What are you doing?' Robert had risen from his chair. 'To whom are you writing?'

Ellen threw a glance at him over her shoulder.

'To Philip, of course,' she replied.

'No, I cannot ask your cousin for favours . . . '

'You don't have to. *I* shall ask him.' Ellen put on her firmest tone, the one she reserved for Jemmy when he had done something naughty, despite repeated warnings not to.

'Yes, but . . . '

'Don't you see, Philip is your best hope? His concern for your sister means he will be as anxious as you that she shouldn't suffer. Moreover, I'm sure he'll lend you his coach and horses on such a mission. Aren't your sister and your mother more important than your wish to be independent?'

For a moment, Robert looked as if he

intended to defy her. Then his shoulders relaxed and his expression softened.

'Thank you,' he said softly. 'You have been a good friend in all of this.'

And Ellen felt her heart both rise and dip like a bird in flight at his last sentence.

10

Events happened almost too quickly for Robert after that. It felt as if hardly any time elapsed between Maggie's departure for the Grange with her mistress's note and the arrival of Philip Longridge in his coach.

The squire had, however, one request to make of Robert in return for lending him his carriage.

'I'd like to go with you,' Philip said. 'I promise I won't get in the way and will let you to speak to your family first, but I can't bear to be left behind, doing nothing.'

There was something fervent about his tone that made it impossible for Robert to refuse. And yet he could not quieten the nagging doubt at the back of his head. He waited till the coach was clear of the steward's cottage before he asked the question that had been haunting him since the previous evening.

'Why didn't you tell me my mother had written to you before she left?'

Philip seemed unable to look him in the eye. He glanced out of the window, then down at his hands. Robert was about to repeat his question when the other man began to speak.

'It was — because of the things she said to me,' he replied. 'She — she said she was sure I would understand why it was necessary for her to remove her daughter from my vicinity, in the same way that she understood that a man in my position could not choose his bride solely according to his fancy. She appealed to my sense of honour and asked me not to try to find them because it would only make things more difficult for myself and for her daughter.'

He looked up suddenly.

'I suppose I could, perhaps should have done as she asked, but — but I could not bear to let Polly go like that.

Not without at least attempting to win her over. I couldn't bear to think of her believing the worst of me — that I was only toying with her feelings while I intended to marry a woman of my own class.'

Robert found himself unexpectedly touched by the other man's emotion, particularly as Philip ducked his head, as if ashamed of having revealed so much.

This is the sort of man I have always wanted for Polly, he realised. *Someone to look after her.* And somehow a yearning thought strayed towards Ellen and Jemmy. If he thought there was a chance, he would fight for them, as Philip was for Polly.

'For what it is worth, I shall champion your cause with my mother and sister,' Robert said.

The eyes of the two men met at last and Philip grasped Robert's hand in a brief but powerful handshake.

'Thank you,' he said. 'That means a great deal to me.'

'Ellen, did you know about this?'

It was just as well she was alone in the parlour, Ellen thought, since Caroline was not even fully inside the room before she began to speak.

'Know about what?' Ellen asked, though she had a fair idea.

'About Philip's dashing off to who knows where with that crippled soldier fellow in search of *that girl.*'

For a second, Ellen toyed with the idea of pretending not to understand this somewhat garbled account, but a glance at her cousin's face told her that, to Caroline, this was no laughing matter. She would not take kindly to being teased.

'I know that, at my request, Philip was generous enough to offer to accompany Mr Lester in his coach to the place where Mrs Lester and her daughter are believed to be residing,' Ellen replied cautiously, but Caroline barely let her finish.

'You *encouraged* this?'

'Why not? Mr Lester has a right to be reunited with his family, especially as he has reason to believe his mother might be gravely ill.'

'Yes, yes, I daresay you meant well,' Caroline conceded impatiently. 'What I meant is that there was absolutely no reason why Philip should go too and you should have told him so in no uncertain terms.'

'I hardly felt it was my place ... ' Ellen began, but Caroline interrupted her.

'You do realise what will happen now, I hope? Philip will fall once more into *that girl's* toils and this time there will be no preventing him from marrying her, though she hasn't a penny to her name and all Philip's fortune will go on maintaining her and her impecunious family and there won't be anything to spare for you or Jemmy ... '

Caroline came to an abrupt halt, but only because she had run out of breath. She seemed so genuinely upset by recent developments that Ellen felt a little sorry for her.

'I'm sure it won't be that bad,' she said, trying not to think about Mr Fairfax's threats.

Caroline uttered a hysterical sob.

'Oh, very good. Bury your head in the sand. It's no skin off my nose. Thank God I have a husband who is capable of providing for me, and any children we may yet have. I don't expect gratitude for all I have done for your benefit. But what am I to do about Amelia? She will be heartbroken if Philip throws her over.'

This was such a surprising statement that it took Ellen a moment to decide from which angle she ought to approach it.

'I don't know why you should talk about Philip *throwing her over*,' Ellen said. 'There has never been an understanding between him and Miss D'Arcy, as far as I can make out. I think if you were to ask your ward for her opinion of your brother, you might discover she has never considered him as a possible suitor. Indeed, she probably regards him as quite middle-aged.'

But Caroline could not be pacified on this score and in the end Ellen decided it was easier to let her cousin pour out all her worries about being thought an unworthy guardian to such an eligible heiress.

'It would have been so perfect — I know I could have trusted Philip to take care of Amelia and her fortune and there would have been enough to spare to maintain you, if you will insist upon remaining at daggers drawn with James's father . . . '

Ellen made a deprecating noise, but in truth she was not concentrating any more, until a sudden sentence jolted her into alertness.

'Even Miss Lester agreed it was the perfect match for Philip.'

'Miss Lester? You've talked to her about this? When?'

Caroline had the grace to blush. But

Ellen did not really need the answer to her question. She knew.

'Just before she and her mother went away,' Caroline replied. She raised her chin defiantly. 'Oh, I know you think I was interfering, but I did it for the best and I wasn't unkind to the girl. I merely pointed out what an unequal match it would be if Philip did make her an offer and what a deal of responsibility it would be for her to have to learn to run such a large household as the Grange when she wasn't brought up to it and she quite agreed with me that it would be unfair of her to stand in the way of Philip's happiness and best interests.'

Ellen thought it prudent not to respond to this in words. She felt even more fellow feeling towards Robert's sister than before, remembering the objections James's father had raised to his son making such a lowly match.

But unlike the Fairfaxes, nobody from my family would ever try to take away any children Polly Lester might have, Ellen thought.

And somehow, for reasons she couldn't quite explain, the image of Robert Lester bouncing Jemmy on his knee flashed across her inner eye.

'Well, it's out of our hands now,' Caroline said with a disconsolate sigh. 'I suppose we shall have to make the best of it.'

Ellen could not suppress a smile. This was typical of Caroline. She might struggle and kick against unwanted changes, but she was on the whole good-natured and if she was allowed to grumble herself calm, she would usually make the best of a bad job.

If only all other problems were so easily resolved.

*   *   *

The house in front of which the coach stopped was humble enough. Clearly it was far older than its nearest neighbours, which dwarfed it almost to the size of a doll's house. But the doorstep had been scrubbed that morning and the windows, which gleamed orange in the afternoon sun, had evidently been recently washed.

Robert glanced at his companion. Philip had been gazing anxiously out of the window, assessing the area of Derby in which they found themselves.

'You'd better go in by yourself,' the latter said, lowering his gaze to look at Robert. 'I'll wait here.'

Robert could see how much this cost him. It was obvious to him that Philip wanted nothing more than to dash into the little doll's house, find Polly and convince her of his love for her.

But Robert's need to find out how his mother was faring — or if she was still alive — had to take precedence over all other considerations.

The journey had been long enough to allow the two men to get to know one another better. But there had also been moments of silence, during which Robert had been unable to stop thinking about Ellen.

Her warning shot through his mind

as he rapped at the door of the diminutive house. Suppose it was a case of mistaken identity? Suppose he still was not at the end of his quest?

The woman who opened the door looked exactly as he had imagined the writer of that letter ought to look. She was round and bustling, with a friendly face and the sort of brisk manner that suggested that there was no difficulty so great that it could not be surmounted in one way or another.

'Mrs Knight?' he asked.

'Yes, sir?'

'My name is Robert Lester. I believe you wrote to me, saying that my mother and sister were lodging in your house?'

Her face lit up, like a sudden shaft of sunlight emerging from a cloud.

'Well, well, little Robin Lester all grown up. I would never have recognised you,' she chirped. 'They *will* be pleased to see you — and Mrs Lester so much better today too. Turned the corner last night, you might say.'

Robert hadn't realised he had been

holding his breath until all the air came rushing out of him. His limbs suddenly felt weak and he could barely propel himself across the threshold straight into the front room of the house.

Indeed, looking around, Robert came to the conclusion that with the possible exception of a pantry or scullery at the back of the house, this was the only room on the ground floor. It was a combination of kitchen and parlour, with something bubbling enticingly in a cauldron above the fire on the wide, old-fashioned hearth, a large kitchen table dominating the far side of the room and a comfortable chair set near the fire for passing long, cold winters' evenings in comfort.

'Perhaps you'd care to wait here while I go and fetch . . . '

But Mrs Knight never got to the end of her sentence. While she was speaking, Robert's ear caught the sound of a light footstep on the staircase, which was tucked into the corner of the room.

'Mrs Knight, I was wondering if the

broth might be ready yet.' A female voice became audible before a slender figure came into view. She stopped abruptly at the sight of Robert.

She had grown thin and pale, with dark shadows smudged beneath her eyes from sleeplessness and anxiety. But the voice was still the same and so was the incredulous smile that spread across her face as her eyes widened.

'*Robert?*' Polly whispered. 'Can it really be you?'

'Yes, it's me.' He smiled back as he limped forward. 'I've come back from the dead.'

And seconds later, Polly had hurled herself against his breast, sobbing out all the pent-up tears she had been careful to suppress during the last dark days because she had known that if she gave way, she wouldn't be able to stop.

★ ★ ★

There did not seem to be words or time enough for all the hasty explanations that followed. To allow brother and sister to speak privately, Mrs Knight had excused herself and nipped surprisingly nimbly up the stairs with a basin of broth for the invalid.

'Don't worry,' she had added with a mischievous twinkle. 'I'll let you break your news to her in your own way.'

It was decided by the two siblings that it might be too much of a shock to their mother if Robert made an appearance unannounced in her bedroom and therefore Polly would go upstairs to break it to her first.

This suited Robert well enough, because there was one other thing he wanted to do in her absence. As soon as she had vanished up the stairs, he turned and hobbled across the room, out of the door and along the street to the coach.

'Won't you come inside?' he said to Philip. 'I think Polly would like to see you.'

He had not told his sister that Philip had come with him to Derby, though he had noticed the way her cheeks flushed and her downcast eyes sparkled when he had told her that Philip had lent him his carriage so he could come and find her and their mother.

Philip demurred, but Robert could see that it wouldn't take much to persuade him to come. At the same time Robert also sensed the other man's nervousness. Now, at last, he was on the brink of achieving what he wanted and he was scared that he might do or say the wrong thing and his dreams would fragment around him, like shards of broken glass.

Mrs Knight was back in the downstairs room when the two men entered. Robert introduced them to one another before he made his cautious way up the staircase. Voices were audible from the backmost of the two small bedchambers whose doors opened onto the small landing.

Robert had turned over several plans about how to persuade Polly to go downstairs without telling her who was

201

waiting for her there, but in the event, it wasn't necessary. After loitering in the bedroom long enough to share the initial hug between them all, Polly drew back voluntarily.

'I'm sure there are things you have to say in private,' she said, though Robert could see how much she wanted to stay, because she still could not quite believe that her brother was alive, if not quite in one piece.

'I might just go out into the yard for a breath of air,' she added hastily and vanished before the others could stop her.

Robert felt a twinge of guilt. Clearly she wanted to be on her own and he had made certain that that would not be possible, or at least not before what might be another emotional or painful scene.

But it was too late to do anything to avert it now and he turned his attention back to his mother. She had aged and her hair had grown greyer since he had last seen her, though he was not sure if time, her recent illness or grief at his supposed death was most to blame for that.

'I can still hardly believe you have come back to us,' she murmured, gazing at his face and clutching his hand tight. 'We didn't want to believe you were dead, not without confirmation, but as the weeks passed and there was no word from you . . . '

'I did write to you as soon as I was well enough to hold a pen. The letter must have gone astray.'

'Yes, of course. I know you would not have left us on tenterhooks deliberately . . . '

And so Robert continued to talk to his mother, trying not to dwell on how ominously silent it had grown in the room below. He had caught the brief, swift rumble of Philip's voice. He thought he had also heard a door open and close almost immediately afterwards and it made his heart heavy to think he had failed.

He should have fulfilled his promise

to Philip and talked to Polly. Now it was too late. Polly must have turned away from Philip, or Philip had given up his suit almost without a struggle and was now waiting for Robert in the coach or taking a stroll around the neighbourhood to work off his feelings.

'Would you open the window?' His mother's voice distracted him. 'I think a breath of air might do me good.'

'Well, if you're sure you won't catch a chill,' Robert said dubiously as he rose and moved towards the window.

What he saw made him stop, however. The yard below was an ugly, utilitarian space, with an outhouse at the far end, damp washing hung out to dry on a line between two wooden posts and a few vegetables and a currant bush growing in a meagre bed.

But Robert doubted that the couple standing there saw any of that. Polly was nestled against Philip's chest, one of his arms wrapped around her, while the other hand had reached tenderly to cup her cheek, as if she was the most

204

precious thing in the world.

For a second, the image of Ellen Fairfax flashed across Robert's mind and all she had done to help him over the last difficult weeks.

But he could not think of such things now.

'There's something I ought to tell you, Mamma,' he said, turning away from the window. 'I did not come here on my own . . . '

★   ★   ★

It would be several days before Mrs Lester would be well enough to make the relatively short journey back to Mansfield, even in the comfort of Philip's coach. Since the steward's cottage was occupied and there was no other house available on his estate, Philip had arranged to hire lodgings above a shop in Mansfield for the whole of the Lester family.

But this was only a temporary arrangement, until all the preparations could be made for Philip's marriage to Polly. Once that was over, Mrs Lester would be able to choose whether to move to the Grange with her daughter or to stay with Robert. He would remain at their lodgings to be close at hand because he had accepted the position as Philip's man of business.

All this Ellen knew from a letter from Philip, which arrived on the day after he and Robert had set out in search of the latter's family. She had scarcely had a chance to read it before the rattle of a carriage announced the arrival of Caroline, who had received a similar missive.

'Really, that brother of mine expects me to arrange it all,' she said, shaking her head. 'He doesn't stop to think I have already promised to help Mrs Marley with the subscription concert and there's Amelia to take care of too and I don't believe my ankle is even half healed yet . . . '

'Oh, don't worry, Caroline,' Ellen reassured her. 'I'll help where I can and so will Miss D'Arcy, I'm sure, if you tell us what to do.'

She cast a humorous smile at Amelia, who was perched somewhat awkwardly on the edge of the couch next to her guardian's wife.

'You always manage everything so splendidly,' Ellen added, knowing that, for all her grumbling, Caroline prided herself on her ability to cope with almost any situation.

It took a little more flattery to mollify Caroline, but as soon as that was done, she proved unstoppable. Ellen was almost sorry she had encouraged her cousin and offered to help. If she wasn't supervising the cleaning of the Lesters' lodgings and the transportation of their belongings to their new home, she was out purchasing what Caroline considered to be the necessities of genteel life ('after all, if the girl is to become mistress of the Grange, we shall have to do *something* to make her fit for the position').

Or else Ellen found herself discussing

whether hothouse flowers at a charitable concert were a necessary expense or an extravagance, or helping Mrs Marley and Caroline to arrange the order in which the amateur musicians were to play in a way that would not offend the sensibilities or pride of rank of any of the performers.

Nonetheless, she was taken by surprise when she arrived at the Grange on the day before Philip and the Lesters were due to return to be greeted in the hall by a distraught Caroline.

'What on earth is the matter?' Ellen asked, as her cousin seized her by both hands.

'Oh, do come into the library for a moment,' Caroline said in an urgent undertone. 'I'm at my wits' end. Whatever shall I do?'

Her eyes looked bloodshot as if, uncharacteristically, she had been crying. A wisp of hair had escaped from her usually smooth knot and it wafted about her ear whenever she moved her head. She shushed Ellen when she tried to ask a question and bustled her out of earshot of the servants into the library, closing the door firmly behind them.

'What *is* the matter?' Ellen persisted, now thoroughly alarmed. 'Has Philip written to you, or — ' She could not think what, other than illness, accident or death, could have caused such distress.

'Philip?' Caroline looked blank for a moment, as if she had never heard the name before in her life. 'No, no, it has nothing to do with him. It's that wretched girl. Whatever am I going to do?'

11

It took Ellen a few seconds to adjust her thoughts.

'I assume by 'that wretched girl', you mean Miss Lester?' she ventured.

'No, no, of course not.' Caroline looked quite cross that she could be so misunderstood. 'I mean Amelia. I swear that girl will turn my hair grey prematurely.'

'Oh.' Ellen could not conceal her bemusement. 'What has she done? Run up excessive debts or — oh, she hasn't eloped with a soldier or some such thing, has she?'

It was Caroline's turn to blink owlishly at her cousin.

'Oh dear, how can you suggest such dreadful things?' she asked and then, catching alarm, she added, 'You haven't heard any rumours, have you? Dear God, it would be too awful — what

210

would society think if — '

She could not bear to finish her sentence, but her eyes widened in horror.

'On top of everything else, it would simply be too dreadful . . . '

It took Ellen several minutes to undo the unfortunate effect of her unthinking suggestions and reassure her cousin that she had heard nothing to the detriment of Amelia's character where financial transactions or affairs of the heart were concerned.

Even then Ellen was not entirely convinced she had succeeded in erasing from Caroline's mind the image of a penniless Amelia escaping through a window into the night with a fortune-hunting redcoat in a post-chaise.

('Because those uniforms *are* very smart and she is *very* young and girls *are* apt to have their heads turned by such superficial things, and it would explain why she was not the least upset when I told her that Philip was to be married . . . ')

At length, Ellen lost her patience.

'Are you never going to tell me what your ward has done to put you in this state?'

Caroline stared at her indignantly.

'But I already *told* you.'

'Indeed you did not, or else I would remember.'

'Oh.' Caroline furrowed her brow. Perhaps she contemplated apologising for the oversight, but if so, she brushed that idea aside. 'Oh, well, after all the efforts I have put in to make the subscription concert a success — and with the programme almost ready to be printed — she has tried to cry off from performing.'

Ellen had not thought it possible for her cousin to take her aback twice in the same morning. Obviously she did not know Caroline as well as she thought she did.

'Is that all?'

'All? *All*? Is that really how you see the matter? After I have told all and sundry how talented she is and what a fine musical education she has received, she — she intends to humiliate me in front of the whole of society. Oh!' She cried out as another thought struck her. 'You don't suppose she intends to elope on the night of the concert and this is a way of ensuring that she'll be able to slip away while everyone is occupied and . . . '

'Caroline, for the last time, as far as I am aware, Amelia D'Arcy is not, nor ever has been, contemplating an elopement.'

'But you said — and there's no smoke without fire — '

'Caroline, there's isn't even the tiniest wisp of smoke. The only gossip I have heard touching Miss D'Arcy concerns the misfortune of her father's death and the fortune she is to inherit as soon as she is of age.'

Caroline subsided and before she could rally, Ellen went on.

'Did Miss D'Arcy give any reason why she does not wish to perform? Perhaps she thinks it is still too soon after her father's death?'

Caroline shrugged helplessly.

'I suppose that may be the reason,' she said grudgingly, 'but if so, she won't talk to me, just says she cannot do it and it would be *cruel* — ' her lips trembled at the word — 'to force her.'

'Oh.'

'Will *you* talk to her?'

'Me?' Ellen couldn't keep the surprise out of her voice.

'Well, you are a little nearer her age than I am and everyone always said you were the musical one in the family.'

Ellen decided it was best to ignore the hint of resentment in Caroline's tone, born of a childhood rivalry which had been fuelled by comparisons made by tactless adults within earshot of the girls. Caroline must have felt it especially galling that all her expensive music lessons and hours of diligent practice were apparently inadequate when compared with Ellen's natural talent, despite the latter's distinct lack of training as her father's profession meant she was hardly ever in one place long enough to hire a piano and engage a music master.

'I don't think my musical talents, such as they are, will bear much weight in this instance,' Ellen began cautiously. But seeing that Caroline still looked a little wild and red-eyed, she relented. 'I don't suppose it could do any harm to talk to Amelia.'

'Oh, thank you, Ellen, you have no idea what this means to me.' Caroline grasped both her hands. 'And while you are about it, I don't suppose you could sound her out about the state of her purse and her heart?'

★　★　★

Ellen found Amelia in the drawing room, whence an indignant Caroline had banished her half an hour earlier, to practise the songs she was to perform at the concert — for perform she must, Caroline had determined, to save their faces in local society.

The girl was sitting disconsolately at the piano, with the sheet music on the stand, but her hands lay limply in her lap. As Ellen opened the door, Amelia started like a pheasant in the under-growth at the sound of a human step.

'Oh, Mrs Fairfax.' She flurried to her feet. 'I did not expect to see you . . . '

'No, well, Mrs Hume asked me to talk to you.'

'Oh.' The girl's face crumpled and Ellen wondered if it had been a mistake to try such a direct approach.

'She's very worried about you,' Ellen said gently. 'We both are. Is it because of your father that you don't wish to perform? Because I am sure people would understand and I may be able to persuade my cousin not to press you to do anything you disliked.'

She tilted her head, but still only had an inadequate view of Amelia's face as the younger woman had dropped her chin onto her breast.

'That's very good of you, madam,' she replied, causing Ellen to wonder when she had become old enough to be addressed so deferentially by a girl of eighteen. 'But — '

'But?'

At last Amelia looked up at her with tear-filled eyes.

'It's not about Papa. Well, maybe just a little,' she amended. 'But — but Mrs Hume has boasted so much about my supposed talents and the songs she has chosen are so difficult and — and I know it's my duty to perform. But — but — '

'But you don't want to fail to do justice to the songs?' Ellen suggested.

'Yes!' Amelia's face lit up, if only for a second.

'Well, if that is all, perhaps we can practise together. And if it really is no good, then I think it is not too late to find some excuse to substitute those songs with some others that you feel more comfortable with.'

Amelia's smile was reward enough to Ellen.

'Oh, thank you, Mrs Fairfax,' she

murmured ardently.

★ ★ ★

Ellen felt tired but satisfied as she made her way back to the steward's cottage. She had spent at least an hour singing with Amelia and discovered to her surprise that Caroline was right. Amelia was far more talented than she gave herself credit for and was perfectly capable of singing the songs her guardian's wife had picked out for her, as long as she was not paralysed by fear.

Ellen suppressed a cough. Nowadays she rarely sang, apart from nonsense songs with Jemmy, and her throat felt parched at the unaccustomed exertion. The thought of Jemmy made her lengthen her stride. She had left him with Maggie, as she often did nowadays, because she never knew what Caroline would expect of her next.

He was in the front garden of the cottage, 'helping' Maggie to water the straggly shoots of the beans, which had

218

just started to poke through the crumbly soil. But as soon as he caught sight of his mother, Jemmy began to totter towards the gate, reaching up with grubby fingers to try to unfasten the latch.

It was as well, Ellen mused, that that was a skill he had not entirely mastered yet, because otherwise she feared they would have had to seek him on numerous occasions in the lane, the neighbouring fields or the grounds of the Grange.

'Come here, my beautiful boy.' Ellen laughed, leaning over the gate in order to hoist him up onto her hip. 'Oof, you're getting big and heavy. Mamma won't be able to carry you much longer. You'll have to carry me instead.'

The very idea made Jemmy chortle infectiously. Ellen prolonged his giggles by tickling him so he squirmed in her arms and tossed his head back so far that for a single terrifying second, Ellen feared she might drop him.

'Have you been a good boy for

Maggie?' she asked, drawing him closer and cradling the back of his head with one hand. 'Have you been helping her with her work?'

She cast a glance at Maggie, who was laughing too.

'Ess. I's a very dood boy,' Jemmy declared emphatically and began listing all the things he had done with Maggie.

While he chattered away, Ellen let herself into the garden. Could anything make this moment any more perfect? As the thought crossed her mind, she had a sudden vision of Robert Lester's face. She knew he too would have appreciated this glorious day and Jemmy's semi-comprehensible chatter.

If only Mrs Lester had recovered faster than anticipated. Then the little party could have set out a day earlier than they had originally planned and . . .

Ellen shook herself. It would be far wiser to enjoy what she had, instead of hankering for the moon. Philip and the Lesters would be back soon enough and with that she would have to be content.

★　★　★

Ellen had just sat down to breakfast the following morning when the carriage arrived. Jemmy was the first to hear it. He abandoned the piece of toast he had been chewing thoughtfully and tilted his head to listen.

'What is it, Jemmy?'

'Unky Phlipip tumming.'

'What makes you say th — ?'

Ellen was brought up short. She could hear it too now. Wheels and hooves. Her heart lifted irresistibly. If it was Philip's carriage, it meant her prayers had been answered and he and the Lesters had either arrived back in Mansfield late the previous evening, or had set out the previous afternoon and slept in an inn on the road.

And although she told herself it could only be Philip on his own — because wouldn't Robert have to make sure his mother and sister were settled in their new home before he went out to visit friends? — her heart soared in anticipation.

Without asking permission, Jemmy had already slid off the edge of his chair and run out of the kitchen, where the little household ate all their meals. With his mother in hot pursuit, he stumbled into the parlour and clambered up onto the windowsill to press his nose against the windowpane.

'Misty Lesty tumming too?' he suggested and his breath instantly misted the glass.

'I don't know, darling.'

Ellen heard the snort of a horse as a carriage stopped at the gate. But as she reached the window, her heart leapt up into her throat. It wasn't Philip's coach, but another vehicle she knew all too well. She snatched up her son, wanting to flee, or pretend she was not at home. But it was too late. Mr Fairfax had already descended from the coach and his sharp eyes had spotted them at the window.

I could lock the door. I could refuse to let him in, send Maggie out through the kitchen window to fetch help from the Grange or the village. I could flee with Jemmy myself, hide myself — where?

She knew the area well enough by now, but the woods were too far away and the Grange too. Mr Fairfax would not demean himself by chasing her himself, but his servants were young, strong and healthy and they knew full well who paid their wages. And the plain truth was that Philip would not be home for several hours yet and there was nobody in the village powerful enough to stand up against Mr Fairfax.

At least this time she was not alone. She refused to move from the spot, so Mr Fairfax would be obliged to knock. She also sent Maggie to open the door.

'Step aside, my good woman. I must speak to your mistress.'

But Ellen knew Maggie's bullish nature well enough to know that these words would only cause her to position herself more squarely in the doorway.

'What name shall I say?'

Despite the seriousness of the situation, Ellen found herself smiling at her maid's impudence. She clutched Jemmy closer and only belatedly noticed that he had left a butter-smear on the white handkerchief fastened round her shoulders.

'Dammit, woman, you know perfectly well who I am,' Mr Fairfax exploded.

Round one to Maggie, Ellen thought, but she was all too conscious of the tremor that had seized her whole body.

'I'm not sure my mistress is at home,' Maggie went on and Ellen realised she was mimicking the servants at Ashton Hall, Mr Fairfax's house, when turning away unwelcome callers.

'Stand aside, woman, or I'll have you arrested for impeding the law.'

The words chilled Ellen to the core. She could not stand by and do nothing.

'Maggie,' she called out, but her voice was nothing but a croak.

Her mind was scrabbling frantically from one thought to another. Surely, surely there was no possibility that it was already done, that Jemmy already belonged legally to his grandfather and not to her. Surely, surely, she should have been informed if legal proceedings had taken place, allowing someone to speak on her behalf, even if she was not allowed to defend herself. Please God, let it all be a bluff.

Don't let this be real. Please make this no more than a nightmare from which I shall wake soon.

But Jemmy's weight dragged on her arms. The morning chill insinuated itself into the house through the half-open front door. The smell of toasted bread still hovered in the air. Surely those things were too ordinary to be part of a nightmare?

Maggie might have been forced to back down, but she still was not prepared to let Mr Fairfax have everything his own way. She obviously insisted on preceding him to the parlour, because she suddenly appeared in the doorway and announced solemnly, 'Mr Fairfax to see you, madam.'

Only then did she stand aside and allow Mr Fairfax to bustle past, though pointedly he made sure that not even his sleeve came into contact with the servant.

Following close behind him was a thinner, weasel-faced stranger whom Ellen had barely noticed as he had slithered out of the coach after Mr Fairfax. Ellen could tell from her father-in-law's impatient, contemptuous look that he expected her to dismiss Maggie. But Ellen set her jaw. Whatever happened in this interview, it would affect Maggie too. And, more than ever, Ellen felt desperately in need of an ally.

She curtsied, taking care to keep her distance from her father-in-law.

'Good morning, sir,' she said, but her voice trembled. 'To what do I owe this . . . ?' But she could not bring herself to utter the words 'pleasure' or 'honour.'

Mr Fairfax cast her a withering look.

'Don't pretend to be as obtuse as your servant,' he replied. 'You know perfectly well why I am here.'

The weaselly man uttered a cough that was clearly meant as some kind of warning to Mr Fairfax. Although Ellen felt her skin crawl instinctively at the sight of this man, she produced her brightest smile.

'You are welcome here, sir, though I am afraid we have not been introduced.'

She was pleased to see the weasel-faced man lose countenance at this, unprepared for her politeness.

'Mr Green is my legal advisor,' Mr Fairfax said stiffly.

'Yes, of course he is.' The words were uttered under her breath. She was not the least surprised. Many lawyers were gentlemen by birth, but something told Ellen that Mr Green had probably clawed his way up from a much lower rank in life by his own efforts.

Ellen was not sure if Mr Fairfax did

not catch her murmur or if he deliberately chose to ignore it.

'I am here, madam,' he said, 'to give you one last opportunity to settle this matter amicably, without resorting to a court of law.'

'This *matter*,' Ellen replied coldly and distinctly, though the tremor still shook her, 'concerns *my son*.'

'And *my* grandson,' Mr Fairfax countered, 'and I think we both know which side the court is likely to favour. Even if by some miracle you were granted custody of the boy, your name would be destroyed by the scandal. You would be ostracised by polite society, no matter who your cousins might be, and I would see to it that not a penny of my fortune would go to you, during my lifetime or after my death.'

'I've told you before, I don't want your money.'

'Nonsense. Everyone needs money. How do you propose to survive?'

Ellen closed her eyes. She knew there was no point in arguing about money with this man. He simply did not understand that not everything and everyone could be bought.

'Isn't it better for the boy that things are settled amicably?'

Ellen's eyes sprang open at the stranger's voice. He had taken two steps towards her and she had not heard him approach.

'If you let him go voluntarily, I will make you an allowance and permit you to visit him twice a year,' Mr Fairfax added. 'But if you fight me over this, I shall make sure you shall never see him again.'

Twice a year. *Twice?* It was an outrage, a violation of all her maternal instincts. She wanted to spurn the offer indignantly.

But she knew, as well as they did, that even with Philip's support, she could not possibly win if the case came before a court. Perhaps if she could stall for time, persuade them that she would consider the proposal, tell them whatever lies were necessary to convince them to leave, so that she and Maggie could pack a few necessities and disappear . . .

And then she looked at their implacable faces. No, there was nothing she could say that would make them trust her.

Twice a year is better than nothing at all, an insidious whisper tickled her ear. *When he is older, you'll be able to explain to him why you were forced to give him up. And when he is a grown man, if he inherits his father's independent spirit, he might even defy his grandfather and come to find you.*

Twice a year, for the next fifteen, seventeen, nineteen years. *How will I bear it?*

'No,' she croaked. 'I can't do it. I can't sell my baby.'

But in all likelihood, neither man heard her last sentence.

'Well, that's unfortunate,' Mr Fairfax said, producing a carefully folded piece of parchment from his coat pocket, 'because I have here a magistrate's order granting me temporary custody of my grandson until the matter can be taken to court.'

12

It was the hardest thing she had ever done. Harder than crossing an ocean with a newborn baby. Harder than searching frantically for news of her husband. Harder even than the dark days after she had accepted the inevitable and had been forced to try to plan a new life for herself and her son.

Because in all those days, she had had Jemmy to care for. His needs had given her life a structure and a purpose. And now what did she have? Only the need to remain as calm as she could, so as not to upset Jemmy any sooner than was necessary.

Mr Fairfax would fain have set out directly, taking none of the little boy's possessions because naturally he could afford to clothe his grandson much more expensively and buy him more elaborate toys. But Ellen had insisted and Mr Green had suggested that maybe 'the child' would have need of a few items on the journey.

Ellen could hardly bear to listen to them. The child, the child. He isn't just *the child*, she wanted to scream. His name is James Fairfax. He's my son. He is a little person in his own right, not a toy to be squabbled over, or a piece of property to be bought and sold, sued and counter-sued for.

But all of that had to be held inside while she packed his clothes with a hard-faced Maggie by her side. She added all but one of the battered toy soldiers to the box and after she had wrapped him up for the journey, Ellen placed Robert Lester's little wooden horse in Jemmy's chubby fist.

'Don't lose that, whatever you do,' she murmured as she struggled for the right words to explain. She pressed her forehead to his so his eyes merged into one. 'Be a good boy and Mamma will do everything she can to get you back, or at least to be allowed to see you now and then.'

Tears contracted her throat, but she blinked and swallowed and tried to smile.

'We dowing to Unky Phlipip's house?' Jemmy asked dubiously.

Ellen shook her head.

'No, you're going to stay with Grandpapa and Grandmamma,' she said, but she sensed that he didn't understand, though he shifted uneasily in her arms.

'Stay with Mamma,' he said.

'No, darling. I'm afraid you can't. But I love you and I always will, even after you've forgotten me.'

Ellen would have stretched out the farewells forever, hoping against hope that Philip and the others might still arrive home sooner than they were expected and would come instantly to the cottage to tell her their news.

But Mr Fairfax was impatient to be gone. As it was, Ellen had the impression that Mr Green had had to restrain him more than once to prevent him from snatching Jemmy out of her arms and marching off with him.

She was glad Mr Fairfax had taken the precaution of bringing a nurse-maid to take care of 'the child' on the journey. She seemed a sturdy, sensible lass, unlikely to panic should a crisis occur, but still she was a stranger and it broke Ellen's heart to be forced to hand over her baby to her. Maggie stroked Jemmy's cheek for the last time and Ellen leaned in to kiss his forehead.

'Mamma tum too?' he asked anxiously.

'No, darling. I'm sorry. I can't. I would if I could.'

Mr Fairfax harrumphed.

'Rather too late for *that*,' he muttered under his breath.

But Jemmy was squirming now, beginning to realise what was happening.

'Mamma tum too,' he insisted as the nursemaid scrambled into the coach after the two gentlemen. 'No!' The panic was audible in his voice. 'Stay with Mamma!'

Maggie uttered a huge sob and Ellen's eyes filled with tears.

'Be a good boy, Jemmy.'

'No, Mamma! Mamma! Stay with Mamma!'

'I love you, Jemmy. I love you.'

She gripped the top bar of the gate, fighting the urge to hurl herself into the coach, wrest her baby free or insist on going with him.

'Mamma!'

The door of the coach slammed, muffling Jemmy's frantic cries, but not eliminating them completely. Ellen could see the nursemaid struggling to keep him in her lap, trying to pacify him with gentle words and hugs, while Mr Fairfax stared stonily into the distance, not even deigning to look at the woman who had once been his daughter-in-law as the coach pulled away from her cottage.

And suddenly, Ellen could not help herself any longer. She threw open the gate and began to run, trying to keep abreast with the window of the coach for as long as she could, not caring about dignity or pride any more.

But all too soon the coach drew away from her and her steps faltered as her breathing constricted. As she was left, panting and sobbing in the country lane, she became aware of a throbbing pain in her left hand. Uncurling her fingers, she found a splinter from the garden gate driven deep into the flesh of her palm. And even that pain was nothing compared with the aching in her breast.

★　★　★

It was strange being back in Mansfield, Robert thought. Philip — he had insisted formalities had to be dropped, at least in private — had brought the Lesters straight to their new lodgings on his way home. But while his mother rested in a comfortable chair by the fire and Polly explored their

237

rooms, exclaiming at the discovery of all sorts of thoughtful conveniences and unexpected luxuries, Robert found himself seized by a strange restlessness.

Perhaps he had been too much cooped up of late, leading a purposeless existence in Derby, waiting for his mother to recover and trying not to get in the way while Philip courted his sister. But at least in Derby he had been able to go out for long walks, to see the sights and build up his strength. Crammed in a coach with his mother and the two lovers, he had felt energy fermenting inside him.

With each milestone they passed, each turnpike they stopped at, each inn at which they changed horses, he whispered silently to himself, I'm going home. I am another mile, another hour, another minute closer to Ellen Fairfax.

'Mamma, would you mind dreadfully if I went for a walk?' he asked abruptly. 'I'm sure Polly will stay with you . . . ' *Please, Polly, stay with her. Please don't ask where I'm going or offer to come with me.* 'I'll try not to be too long . . . '

How long would it take him to walk to the steward's house, exchange a few words with Ellen and Maggie, give Jemmy the splendid new top he had bought in Derby and show him how to make it spin?

'Well, of course, if that is what you wish,' his mother replied, but she was obviously puzzled by his mood.

He could not bring himself to explain.

'Bless you, Mamma. Behave yourself and do everything Polly tells you.'

'Oh, you . . . '

Mrs Fairfax pretended to take a swipe at him as he hurried past.

It was not an ideal arrangement, Robert thought, pulling a wry face as he manoeuvred down the staircase. But he was sure that the rooms were the best that could be procured at such short notice.

The day was quite advanced by now,

though the evenings were growing longer now that spring had well and truly set in. He could not help comparing this fine, blustery afternoon with the day he had first returned from America, completely unaware that such a person as Ellen Fairfax existed.

Now the hedgerows were flourishing, the hawthorns a mass of white blossom while violets and forget-me-nots created banks of colour amid the lush grass.

Robert couldn't help pausing at the cottage gate to admire the still-pale shoots and tiny leaves that had begun to emerge in neat rows in the kitchen garden. His head shot up as he heard the door spring open and a woman's steps running towards him.

But his joyful smile froze to his lips. It was not Ellen, but Maggie, looking more distressed than he had ever seen her.

'Maggie, what is it?' And almost instantly, he thought he knew. 'Jemmy?'

Maggie uttered a sob that confirmed his darkest fears.

'When did it — how did it — how is Ellen bearing up?'

He didn't even notice that he had used her first name.

'Just this morning. The fiend had been to a magistrate behind Miss Ellen's back, didn't even give her a chance to say her piece — oh, I could have strangled him with my bare hands.'

'Mr — Mr Fairfax was here?' Robert's heart thudded insistently.

He had been so terrified that Jemmy had been taken ill or had an accident while they were away. He knew he ought to have been relieved that the little boy was alive and well, but it only seemed to open another chasm before his feet — that of Ellen's grief. How would she survive without her beloved son?

'He brought his lawyer with him too, to make sure it was all legal,' Maggie went on bitterly, barely seeming to hear Robert's words. 'And a nursemaid too, because heaven forefend that he should have anything more to do with his grandson than paying the bills.'

'And you say this happened this morning?'

'Aye, aye, just . . . I don't know — seven, eight hours ago maybe.'

Robert groaned and closed his eyes. If only they had set out yesterday. They had discussed the possibility, but ultimately decided against it because of his mother's health. As it was, they had only stopped to change horses and feed themselves.

And now it was too late. He could not spool back time, do things differently, achieve a different outcome. His logical mind told him, legally, there was nothing they could have done to prevent Mr Fairfax from claiming his grandson. From the little he had seen of the elderly squire, Robert guessed he would have made sure no precaution had been left untaken.

But in his heart, he felt they might have done something, he and Philip and maybe Maggie too. Between them, they might have been able to persuade Mr Fairfax to relent, or kept him distracted while Ellen made her escape with Jemmy or — or *something*.

They had known Mr Fairfax was a threat. Why had they allowed Ellen to stay in the cottage? If she had been living at the Grange with Caroline Hume and her husband and all the servants, then perhaps this disaster might have been delayed, if not entirely averted. Instead they had both been too self-absorbed: he worried about his mother, while Philip was anxious to find Polly again.

All the while Maggie had been talking, talking. Letting out all the words that had been pent up since morning. All the things Robert knew instinctively she had not been able to say to Ellen because she had had to remain strong for her mistress, even though she adored Jemmy as much as if he was her own flesh and blood.

'I should've insisted, as soon as he found out where we was. I should have

243

taken her and the little fellow to stay with my sister.'

'Don't, Maggie. Don't torment yourself. There's nothing you could have done. Mr Fairfax would have found you sooner or later.'

She shook her head, but Robert went on before she could say any more.

'The most important thing is to help Mrs Fairfax. How is she? Where is she?'

'She — she's inside,' Maggie replied, swallowing another sob. 'She — oh, I've never seen her like this, not even when the captain died. I haven't dared leave her, even to go and talk to Mrs Hume. She's just lying there on her bed, her eyes blank and tearless, as if she'll never cry again — it'd break my heart, if it hadn't been smashed to pieces already. It's as though she's given up all hope of ever seeing her son again.'

'Oh.'

Again Robert closed his eyes, desperately trying to think what he ought to do.

'Would — would you talk to her, sir?'

Maggie asked, uncharacteristically timidly. 'If you'd just stay with her for a little while, I'd nip to the Grange and tell them what's happened.'

Robert knew all the arguments against it. If the likes of Mrs Marley discovered he had been alone with Ellen in her bedroom, he knew she would jump to the wrong conclusions. But he didn't care. He *wanted* to be the one to console Ellen — if he could.

'Yes, of course. I'll go to her at once. You do what you must. Perhaps Mr Longridge will be able to find a way to — ' He broke off, but Maggie nodded, just as eager as he was to cling to some hope, however remote or flimsy it might be.

It gave Robert an eerie feeling to open the front door and enter that house alone. Being back in his former home reminded him that his mother and sister would wonder what had become of him. But he knew they would forgive his absence once he had explained.

He glanced into the parlour and the kitchen, just in case Ellen had come downstairs while he had been talking to Maggie. Then he paused in the hall. The tiny cottage was as silent as if it had been completely abandoned. A dart of fear shot through him, though he did not quite dare put that fear into words.

He wanted to dash upstairs, as he would have done as a boy. The need to be careful annoyed him. Nor could he move silently. Ellen must have been aware of his presence in her house, and moreover, be able to identify him from the wooden thunk of his leg and crutches. It frightened him that she did not come out to intercept him.

He limped past the room that had once been his and pushed open the door of Ellen's room. Panic seized him. There was nobody there, though the rumpled coverlet suggested someone had been lying on top of the bed.

For a moment, Robert stayed motionless, as if he believed that if he stared long enough at the bed, Ellen would appear. Then he turned and hurried on. There was only one more room on this floor, the tiny chamber Jemmy had shared with Maggie while he was still too small and too unpredictable to be trusted to sleep on his own.

Hardly daring to breathe, Robert pushed open the door. His eye fell instantly upon the empty cot by the low-set window under the sloping ceiling. He pushed the door a little wider.

Ellen was curled up on the floor beside the cot, her head on the little pillow. The hand furthest from him was wrapped in a white bandage and curled into a fist. She did not move and for a frantic moment, Robert wondered if she was even alive.

But as he lowered himself down to the floor beside her, she lifted dead eyes to his face.

'He's gone,' she said.

'I know. I'm sorry.'

The words sounded so pathetically

inadequate. She was gazing at him, as if he could offer her some desperate hope.

'How will I endure it?'

'I don't know. I don't know. I'm so sorry.'

He let instinct take over as he gathered her to his breast, rocked her against him, stroked the unravelled strands of her long, dark hair while she clung to him and cried as if she would never stop. Unable to resist, he let his lips brush softly against her forehead and he felt her shudder in his arms. But she made no attempt to break free.

'Maybe — maybe it's not all over. Maybe there's some way we can make things better. Some way we can soften Mr Fairfax's heart,' he murmured, because he could not bear to hear her gasping for breath with the intensity of her grief. 'Maybe somehow . . . '

She shook her head against his shoulder, but made no other protest.

Afterwards Robert was not sure how long he spent crouched beside Ellen, next to Jemmy's bed. The room grew dusky as her sobs became ragged and painful and still he dared not move because he did not want to let her go.

He had not realised she had lapsed into a drowse until one of her hands dropped lifelessly from his shoulder into her lap and he saw her half-curled fingers still clutched a battered toy soldier.

13

It was the sound of the front door that woke Ellen from her drowse. Jolted out of her moment of oblivion, she suddenly became aware of whose shoulder she had been nestled against, whose arms were wrapped round her back, whose fingers rested amongst her dishevelled hair. Whose kiss still tingled on her forehead.

'I'm sorry,' she murmured, not daring to meet Robert's eye as she gently disentangled herself and scrambled to her feet. 'I didn't mean to give way like that.'

'Ellen, how could you *not* give way? You had every right to cry and I — I was glad to be of some use when I have failed so signally to protect you or your son.'

She was startled to hear her name upon his lips, but she had no wish to chide him for it. Instead, she shook her head.

'You mustn't blame yourself. I am not your responsibility and neither is Jemmy.'

Her voice, which had sounded oddly blank, even to her own ears, wobbled on the last word. She swallowed hard. Robert was struggling to lever himself upright and she forced herself to step forward to help. She felt a dart of lightning as his fingers curled round her shoulder. He tottered and instinctively she wrapped her arm around his waist.

'Mrs Fairfax? Mr Lester? Are you there?' Maggie called cautiously from the landing, as if afraid of disturbing a sleeper.

Ellen's eyes met Robert's, but he seemed less perturbed than she was at the thought of being caught so close together.

'Just coming,' he called back.

'How is she?' Philip's voice called from further away and Ellen heard him thundering up the stairs, two at a time.

251

It reminded her of the visits she used to pay her cousins, when they were all children. Like most boys, Philip had done almost everything in a rush.

'I'm — ' she could not lie — 'as well as can be expected,' she amended.

The door burst open. Maggie must have stepped aside to allow Philip to pass her on the landing because suddenly he was standing before her, his hat clutched in his hand.

'Oh, Ellen, I'm so dreadfully sorry. I should have taken steps to protect you both before I went gallivanting off. I should at least have insisted that you come and stay at the Grange.'

Ellen shook her head and again the ache inside her welled up so it was all she could do not to double up.

'It doesn't matter. It would have made no difference. He'd gone to a magistrate . . . '

'And told some unforgivable lie about your suitability to take care of Jemmy,' Philip broke in with uncharacteristic vehemence. Ellen was so used to him appearing calm and in control of his emotions that it was unsettling to see him like this.

But she merely shrugged.

'Perhaps. But it's too late now.'

'We'll see about that. I've already sent one of the grooms to fetch my attorney.'

Ellen felt a flicker of hope, but she forced herself to douse it. She could not afford to let herself hope. Not yet. Not when there was no immediate prospect that she would not be left more crushed and bereaved than ever by having her worst fears confirmed.

'You mustn't be downhearted, Ellen. We'll do everything that is humanly possible to reunite you with Jemmy . . . '

'Please, Philip, don't. I can't bear it. Not now.'

Her cry of pain echoed in the tiny chamber and all of a sudden she felt trapped and enclosed.

'I'm sorry,' she said. 'Let's go downstairs. Perhaps Maggie can make some tea . . . '

She didn't want tea. The very thought of it made her feel sick. But for the moment, she had to get them all out of that little room.

'Of course. Anything you want.'

Not *what I want. I only want one thing and that is impossible.*

But she followed them out onto the landing, closing the door behind her. She did her duty, put on a brave face, tried not to choke over her tears when she caught a sympathetic look from one of the others. Tried to convince the men that there was nothing they could have done, even if they had been home when Mr Fairfax arrived. Reassured them that she did not blame them for anything that had happened, even though perhaps she did a little.

When at last the men realised how late it was and that both of them had families waiting for their return, Ellen heaved a surreptitious sigh of relief. She knew they meant well, but it was such a strain, trying to maintain the façade. Alone with Maggie, there would be no need for her to pretend any more.

The look Robert gave her as she rose to escort them to the door almost reduced her to tears again. His gaze was too tender, too sympathetic. It reminded her again of what she had lost.

At the door, after they had said their farewells, Philip turned back one last time.

'Why don't you come with me, Ellen? You'll be more comfortable at the Grange and I don't like leaving you on your own.'

'I'm not on my own. Maggie will be here with me. And I — I don't think I am quite ready yet to face Caroline and the others.'

'Of course.'

But he didn't know that wasn't the real reason, though it was true Ellen dreaded encountering her other cousin at present. The real reason why she could not leave the steward's cottage was because the worst had already happened. It was too late for a change of lodgings to protect her.

And this was the only place in the neighbourhood where she could be alone with her memories of Jemmy, the bed in which he had slept, the stairs he had tumbled down, the chair he had sat on with his feet dangling well clear of the floor. At present, there was nowhere else she wanted to be.

★   ★   ★

Her recovery was painfully slow. For days, Jemmy's last calls echoed in her ears. In her nightmares, she saw his little face at the window of the coach, his hands scrabbling frantically, trying to get free.

Does he cry himself to sleep at nights? Does he call for me, or Maggie? Is he angry because I have abandoned him? Are they angry with him because he calls for me? How can I bear it?

All she wanted to do was cry and mope about the house or obsessively trace the paths where she and Jemmy had taken their walks.

But life and its rhythms reasserted itself. Philip arrived on her doorstep on the day after Jemmy's departure, to tell her what his lawyer had said about challenging Mr Fairfax's claim of custody. It was as she had thought. The chances were extremely slim, but Philip was not prepared to give up until they had examined every single loophole in the law that could reunite her with her son.

He also insisted on whisking her to the Grange, where Caroline awkwardly expressed her sympathy and then applied her solution to all heartache — solid, hard work.

'The preparations for Philip's wedding won't arrange themselves,' Caroline pointed out. 'And I am not at all sure this house is quite as it should be to receive a new mistress, no matter how humble her background might be.'

She evidently had not quite forgiven Polly or Philip for their engagement, though Ellen could see she was doing her best to be magnanimous.

Amelia too was sympathetic, though in a less brisk fashion, and as for Mrs Lester, at Ellen's first meeting with her cousin's future mother-in-law, the older woman grasped her in a warm embrace.

'I can't imagine what you must be suffering now,' she murmured. 'I'm sure I should have run mad if anyone had tried to steal either of my children, especially when they were so small.'

For Robert's sake, Ellen did her best to befriend his sister and protect Polly from Caroline's determined efforts to transform her into a lady. Fortunately, despite being several years younger than Polly, Amelia took her under her wing. So while Caroline did her best to instil in Polly all the necessary knowledge to become the mistress of the Grange, Amelia accompanied them to the best mercers' shops in Nottingham and helped choose patterns for the new clothes Polly would need.

It meant that Ellen was allowed to retreat gratefully into the background, to help Mrs Lester with the more humble preparations for the wedding, like ordering food and making sure the house was in good order.

There was something very soothing about being with the older woman. She was quite willing to sit in companionable silence with Ellen while they embroidered Polly's initials onto the household linen, away from the bustle of the wedding preparations that only served to remind Ellen of how much she had lost.

Robert came across them one afternoon, sewing in the smaller parlour at the Grange, where they both felt more at ease than in the large, formal drawing room.

'I see you're working hard,' he said. 'I called in at the cottage on my way homeward and Maggie told me I would find you here.'

Ellen did her best to return his smile.

'Was there anything in particular you wanted?' she asked.

'No, no, I just wanted to see how you

were. I feel as if I have barely seen you during the last days.'

Ellen knew that he too had been very busy, familiarising himself with the way the Grange's estate was run and acting as an intermediary between landlord and tenants. Since the locals all remembered Robert's father, they tended to think of him as one of their own and therefore easier to approach with their concerns than a well-bred outsider like the squire.

Philip had more or less permanently lent Robert one of his horses, as he could not afford to keep one himself. It meant that Robert could travel much further afield on business and his leisure hours were scarce.

They had almost caught up on their news when there was an explosion of female voices in the entrance hall. A moment later, Caroline burst into the parlour, with Amelia and Polly trailing in her wake, giggling like schoolgirls.

'So this is where you've been hiding yourselves,' Caroline remarked. 'I don't suppose you know where my husband and my brother are?'

Ellen shook her head. 'They went out for a walk after dinner and I haven't seen either of them since.'

'Oh, no matter. I'll talk to them later, I daresay.' Caroline dropped gratefully into an armchair. 'Well, at least that's done. I don't think we'll have to go to Nottingham again before the wedding.'

'I hope you haven't put yourself out too much on Polly's account,' Mrs Lester ventured. She was still not entirely comfortable with addressing Philip's family as equals, though Ellen had discovered she had an understated sense of humour.

'Oh, it's no trouble.' Caroline dismissed her words with a wave of the hand. 'Appearances must be maintained and all that.'

'Besides which, Caroline likes to be asked for her advice,' Ellen added, earning herself an exasperated glare from her cousin.

'I did tell Mrs Hu — Caroline how

261

grateful I was.' Polly also felt the need to chime in. 'So many pretty things — far too many and far too pretty for me.'

Her last words elicited protests not only from Caroline, but from Amelia too. But as packages were opened to allow those who had stayed behind to admire the purchases, Ellen felt herself slipping from the scene, as if she was observing it from a vast distance. As if she did not belong to this world any more.

'And this is for you, Ellen.' Caroline's voice roused her abruptly. 'It's about time you started wearing colours again.'

The parcel was in Ellen's lap before she could react. Her sense of alienation only seemed to increase. The bolt of silk was deep midnight blue. She knew she ought to be grateful that Caroline had not chosen something garishly bright or girlishly pretty. She knew her cousin only had the very best of intentions. But it felt as if Caroline was trying to negate her past, erase James and perhaps

Jemmy too, by offering her new clothes, a new life, even a new identity.

'Thank you,' she said with an effort. 'It's beautiful.'

'Of course with your colouring, you could afford to wear much brighter colours,' Caroline said. 'But in the circumstances, I thought it better . . . '

'Yes, of course.'

Please, Caroline, don't say any more, Ellen begged. *I'm not sure I could bear it.*

But just as Caroline was opening her mouth, Robert cut in.

'Did you also have rain in Nottingham?' he asked. 'I got caught in a shower halfway between two of the most remote farmhouses on the edge of Sherwood Forest . . . '

Caroline seized on the topic of the weather with such enthusiasm that Ellen suspected she too was relieved at the change of subject. Ellen flashed a grateful smile at Robert and he inclined his head ever so slightly in acknowledgement.

Even so he took her by surprise when she suggested it was time for her to leave.

'Perhaps I might be permitted to escort you home?'

'Of course, if you wish,' she replied. 'But are you not tired after your long day?'

He pulled a rueful face.

'I've been in the saddle all day and should like to stretch my legs a little,' he said. 'Besides, I hope you will temper your pace to mine.'

A smile came unbidden to Ellen's lips.

'I think I can manage that,' she said.

But once they were alone, strolling through the gardens of the Grange, neither of them seemed to know what to say.

'I wish — ' Robert began, before stopping himself.

'Yes?' Ellen asked, a strange sensation in her breast. As if, she didn't know quite how, something hopeful or good might occur.

'I hope the frivolity of the others just now did not upset you,' he ventured and Ellen had the strangest feeling that he had changed what he had originally intended to say.

She shook her head. 'No, it's nice to see other people enjoying themselves,' she said. 'I would not wish to impose my gloom on everybody else.'

She dropped her head so he would not see that her eyes had darkened. A long sigh seeped out of her companion.

'I wish there was something I could say or do that would make things better,' he said. 'I hate seeing you like this.'

'Oh, don't worry about me. I'm sure I'll survive.' Again she tried to smile, but she was not sure how well she succeeded. 'After all, one day, Jemmy will be old enough to be independent of his grandfather. All I have to do is w — '

Her voice faltered on the last word. Waiting for years, perhaps decades. And even then there was a danger that

Jemmy's mind might be poisoned against her, or that he might be angry that she had apparently given him up without a fight, because he was too young to understand or remember anything that happened now.

'It won't take that long.' There was something fierce about Robert's voice. 'I swear it. Somehow, I will get Jemmy back for you.'

Ellen thanked him, but it must have been obvious to him that she did not believe it was possible. He did not pursue the subject. They said their farewells at the cottage gate and Ellen paused on her doorstep, to watch him wending his sad way back to the house to collect his mother and sister.

Perhaps he sensed her gaze. He turned his head back. Their eyes met for a moment longer and he raised one arm to wave. She returned the wave, then turned away into the darkness and eerie quiet of the house.

As she entered her parlour, her eye

was irresistibly drawn to a simple brown jug on the windowsill, containing a dozen butter-coloured daffodils.

'Oh, how pretty,' she exclaimed instinctively.

'Mr Lester brought them for you,' Maggie replied. 'Seems to me he's quite taken with you.'

But Ellen made no reply.

14

'I'm glad you decided to come,' Robert Lester said. 'I hope you will keep us in countenance, so we can all be outcasts together.'

Ellen could not help laughing faintly at that, the first time she had mustered more than a smile since Jemmy had been snatched from her. All the same, it was with some trepidation that she followed the rest of her party into the Assembly Room adjoining the Town Hall.

It was the night of the charity concert and the whole of local society had turned out in its finest apparel. As she nodded politely to acquaintances, Ellen was well aware that their party was attracting a good many stares and whispers, though it was not clear whether the loss of her son, the squire's intended misalliance with the former steward's daughter or Robert's miraculous return from the dead excited them most.

Ellen knew that both her family and Robert's had tried to protect her from Mrs Marley and her cronies, all of whom were agog at the latest scandal connected with the mysterious Mrs Fairfax.

It was only belatedly that Ellen realised that they were inclined to take the gossip at face value and assume that her father-in-law must have had good reason to lay claim to his grandson in such a fashion. If Ellen had not been so closely related to the new squire and his sister, she might have found herself ostracised by polite society.

'Not that I would care much for that in the ordinary way,' Ellen had confided in Maggie. 'But Caroline is insisting that I *must* go to the concert and all the others agree.'

'Of course you must go,' Maggie had replied stoutly. 'You can't let those petty-minded tattle-mongers defeat you. What would the captain have said?'

Ellen groaned.

'Not you too.'

The truth was, Ellen knew the story could be twisted in either way. If she went to the concert, she might be considered to be flaunting herself heartlessly, even after the loss of her son. Stay at home and it would be whispered that she had finally accepted that she was not a fit person to be admitted into respectable society. In the end, it was Amelia's pleas that had swayed her. The girl was clearly still terrified of performing in public, despite Ellen's attempts to bolster her confidence.

Philip had suggested that they should come in two carriages — his own and his brother-in-law's — so that they could collect the three Lesters along the way. Philip himself led the way into the Assembly Room, with Mrs Lester on his arm, followed by Caroline and her husband with Amelia and Polly.

Ellen brought up the rear with Robert Lester, who looked somewhat self-conscious in the scarlet coat of his former regiment. It had been cleaned and made as presentable as possible for the occasion, but it still showed signs of wear.

'My mother insisted I had to wear it,' he confided to Ellen.

'And quite right too, considering who will benefit from this charitable endeavour,' Ellen replied, imitating Caroline's intonation in order to make him laugh.

And then the thought of the widows and orphans of dead soldiers inevitably made her think of Jemmy and James and the smile drained from her face.

To her surprise, Robert squeezed her hand.

'Don't give up hope,' he said and she was forced to blink back a sudden tear.

Philip ensured they had prominent places, as befitted the party of the local squire. Glancing along the row of seats, it struck Ellen that Amelia was looking rather pale. She had fallen silent, despite Polly's attempts to cheer her, and Ellen regretted that she was seated too far away to be able to offer any words of encouragement.

She offered up a silent prayer when it came to Amelia's turn to perform. Ellen touched the heiress's arm lightly as she passed her, but Amelia only managed the faintest twitch of a smile in response.

Ellen felt her stomach clench as Amelia sat down at the piano and spread out her skirts. But after a brief hesitation, she played the introduction, a little more shakily than in the drawing room at the Grange, it was true, but with only one false note.

Ellen relaxed momentarily. And then Amelia opened her mouth and not a single sound emerged. She came to a stumbling halt in her accompaniment and her face flushed crimson as she ducked her head.

There was a stir throughout the Assembly Room. Ellen did not stop to think. Acting on impulse, she rose, murmuring an apology to Robert as she pushed past him into the aisle. She reached the piano just as Amelia was rising from the stool.

'I'm sorry. I can't — ' she murmured, clearly wanting to flee from the scene of her humiliation.

'Of course you can do it,' Ellen replied, taking her by both hands. 'But if you don't trust your voice, then just play the accompaniment and I'll sing it for you.'

She met the girl's frightened gaze as fearlessly as she could and she felt some of the tension trickle out of Amelia's body.

'Would you?' she breathed.

'Of course.'

'Thank you.'

It was only a whisper, but Amelia sank back onto the stool. Ellen positioned herself behind her, where she could see the music. Though if she was truthful, she had also chosen this position so she would not be obliged to look at the audience directly. The onlookers were growing more restless and noisy by the minute.

Someone uttered a sibilant 'Hush!' and the noise subsided. But Ellen was grateful that Amelia began the accompaniment before the room fell completely silent because otherwise they might both have lost their nerve.

Mercifully, after all the practice with Amelia lately, Ellen's voice was stronger and more flexible than it had been for some years. She was relieved that Amelia elected to sing too. As her confidence increased and her voice grew in power, Ellen reined in her own singing, allowing Amelia to shine in her full glory.

When stunned silence gave way to enthusiastic applause, Ellen stood aside, so Amelia could take centre stage. Ellen had tried hard not to pick out any faces amid the crowd, but as she glanced up, she found herself lost in Robert Lester's gaze. He was looking at her with such warmth and admiration that she felt utterly overwhelmed.

She seemed to be floating on a cloud as she made her way back to her seat. And yet even in this dazed, blissful state, the outer world had the power to crush her.

She heard a pointed sniff from one of the seats she passed and the deliberately overloud whisper, 'Of course, her kind will always do anything to attract attention to themselves.'

It's no use. I can never win. She closed her eyes as she sank into her seat, to hold back tears of exhaustion.

Her whole body tingled as a large, masculine hand gently took hold of hers and Robert's voice tickled her earlobe.

'That was a beautiful thing you did for Miss D'Arcy,' he said. And he refused to release her hand until she had looked up at him and returned his smile.

★   ★   ★

The wedding of Philip Longridge, Esq. and Miss Mary Lester, Spinster, took place three days after the concert. It was meant to be a quiet ceremony, involving only the families of both parties. For that reason alone, Philip had taken care to obtain a special licence, rather than having banns read on three successive Sundays.

But as Ellen pointed out to him, nothing could really be kept private and small when Mrs Marley was involved. As the wife of the vicar, it was impossible that she would fail to sniff to the news. And, of course, there was only one thing that a gossip could do with such a juicy titbit.

As a result, the churchyard and the main street of the village were lined with well-wishers, who had been unable to take the whole day off work, but who still wanted to see the squire and his bride in all their finery. Robert Lester limped down the aisle to give away his sister and, at her own request, Amelia D'Arcy acted as Polly's bridesmaid.

('A true sign of the world turned upside down,' Mrs Marley opined to her husband later in the privacy of her own parlour.)

Much to the disappointment of the curious, the Longridges and Lesters then retreated to the Grange for a celebratory dinner *en famille*, though at the squire's expense, several casks of ale were provided and two sheep were roasted on the village green for all to partake in.

'I see you wore your new gown,' Robert remarked to Ellen at the dinner table.

All day it had seemed to her there had been a suppressed excitement about him, as if he knew a secret he had been forbidden to tell.

'It seemed like an appropriate occasion,' she replied. 'Black at a wedding felt wrong — as if I meant to curse the bride and groom.'

'Well, your cousin has exquisite taste,' he said. 'You look beautiful.'

Ellen knew he was flattering her, and yet she could not help smiling and blushing like a schoolgirl. She was relieved, however, that Caroline's husband Jonathan chose that moment to call for a toast to the bride and groom, which everyone seconded vigorously. Philip thanked them and proposed another toast.

'To the most beautiful bride in the world!'

There was a chorus of approval as Polly ducked her head to hide her blushes.

'May your union be long and fruitful,' Caroline added, not to be outdone, but undermined the effect she was trying to create by casting a dubious glance at Ellen.

Ellen forced a brilliant smile to her lips and raised her glass to the happy pair.

'May you have dozens of happy, healthy children,' she said and was proud that her voice did not wobble.

'I'm not sure I can afford quite that many,' Philip pretended to grumble, but raised his glass nonetheless.

There were too few of them to form a

longways set for dancing after dinner, but Philip insisted that there had to be parlour games and riddles of all sorts. Even Caroline forgot her dignity and consented to join in, revealing a hitherto unsuspected knack for inventing ingenious forfeits for the others to pay, while Mrs Lester's riddles were declared to be so inventive as to be almost unsolvable.

Ellen resolutely pushed away sad thoughts, determined not to spoil the day for the others, but inevitably towards evening, she began to flag. It was Robert who sensed the change in her mood and picked a moment when everyone else was distracted to ask if she would prefer to go home.

'I'm sure the others would understand,' he added.

Somehow it seemed inevitable that he would walk her home, even though she protested that nothing much could go amiss on such a short journey. But Robert was adamant and, she realised, she *wanted* him to come. It would have been too melancholy walking back alone through the twilight.

Only Mrs Lester glanced up as they slipped out of the door and Ellen blushed as she caught the older woman's knowing smile.

'So,' Robert broke their silence after a while, 'how are you?'

She could sense what he really wanted to ask, but dared not voice.

'It's been a good day,' she said. 'Of course, I'd be lying if I said it hadn't brought back memories, but I think it's done me good to have something else to think about, at least for a little while.'

'Good. I'm glad.' But there was a slight reservation in his tone.

'I hope Philip and Polly will be as happy as I was with James,' Ellen went on. 'Oh, I am not saying that we never quarrelled or that there weren't times when I didn't long for a home of my own, especially after Jemmy was born. But still I would not have missed it for the world.'

Robert had bowed his head and Ellen

had the impression it was not solely because he was having to pick his way forward carefully in the fading light.

'Would you ever consider — no, it's a foolish question,' he broke off, but Ellen felt a prickling along her spine. 'Please, forget I said anything.'

'Would I ever consider marrying again? Is that what you meant to ask?'

His head dipped lower and he bit his lip. She knew she was right and before he could deny it, she went on.

'If you had asked me that a year ago, I would have said no,' she said. 'But just recently, before Jemmy was taken away from me, I was beginning to think — maybe.'

It felt very forward, as if she was throwing herself at him. She blushed, remembering his spontaneous proposal. She had thought at the time it was only a reaction to the threats of her father-in-law. But there had been moments when she had wondered whether there might not be more to it than that.

On the other hand, she did not want to put Robert in an awkward position if she had misunderstood his intentions.

Slowly he raised his head. Their eyes met.

'Ellen,' he began and another shiver passed down her spine. When he uttered her name, it almost sounded like music. 'There's something I must tell you. I can't keep silent any longer . . . '

He was cut short by the thud of hooves. They started apart, as if they had been caught in a misdeed and turned their heads towards the source of the noise. Ellen felt her heart being clenched in a vice. They had only just left the wedding party. Surely no disaster could have occurred so soon?

In the dim light, it was not until the carriage pulled up alongside them that she recognised the coat-of-arms emblazoned on the door.

'Oh God, what now?' she groaned, despair gripping her. 'They've already taken all that is most precious to me.

What more can I be expected to give?'

Robert tucked one crutch more firmly under his arm so he could free his hand and reach out to touch her arm.

The coachman had already leapt down from his box.

'Urgent letter for Mrs James Fairfax,' he said.

Ellen felt herself shrinking, not wanting to confront whatever this was. It struck her as odd that Mr Fairfax had gone to the expense of sending a letter in this manner, when it would have been quicker to send a messenger on horseback.

For Jemmy's sake, I must know the worst, she told herself, taking the letter and breaking the seal before she could change her mind.

But the news was far worse than even she had dared anticipate.

15

She closed her eyes and swayed.

'Ellen!'

The cry cut through the swirl in her brain. She fought with every ounce of her strength to remain conscious and clear-minded. She felt the nails of one hand dig into her palm while the letter rustled in the other hand.

'What's happened? What further outrage has that man perpetrated against you?'

Ellen shook her head, dissipating the dregs of faintness. Opening her eyes, she saw that Robert seemed torn between watching her solicitously and glaring at the coachman, as if he were to blame for the message he had brought.

'It's — it's Jemmy,' Ellen said. 'He's — he's been taken dangerously ill and — and he's been asking for me.'

'They've sent for you?' Robert whispered incredulously.

Ellen nodded, her throat suddenly so full that she could not speak. She did not know how to feel. Her baby was ill and she was so far away, but she would be allowed to see him again, if only for a little while — but only if she got there before it was too late.

'I've instructions to take Mrs James Fairfax back with me to Ashton Hall,' the coachman confirmed.

'I must tell Maggie and pack a few things for the journey,' Ellen said, stirring herself into action. She turned towards the coachman. 'Perhaps you'd like to step inside and have a bite to eat and a sup of ale while you wait? I won't be long.' Another thought struck her, as she was about to hurry away. She glanced at Robert. 'Oh, you will tell Philip where I've gone, won't you?'

'Of course,' Robert began, but cut off the last word halfway. 'No. I'll write a note and we can leave it at the Grange in passing, but I can't let you go alone.

I'm coming too.'

'Oh, but I can't impose on you like that,' Ellen protested as he bustled her towards the house.

'Nonsense. I love Jemmy too, you know. I couldn't bear not knowing how he is and having to wait for you to send word or come back ... ' His voice trailed away. He resumed more briskly, 'Now, you go and tell Maggie what to pack while I write a note to Philip and another to my mother.'

Since there was not a moment to be lost, Ellen obeyed, though she had no intention of letting him come, tempting though his offer was. To her surprise, however, Maggie took Robert's side.

'Wouldn't trust those Fairfaxes further than I could kick them,' she declared. 'Besides, you never know what dangers you might encounter on the road. And don't think you're leaving me behind either, because I'm not having any of it. The cottage'll come to no harm, even if it is left locked up for a while.'

And so it was that within half an hour, the coach had set out again, now bearing not only Ellen, but Maggie and Robert as well. They stopped twice more before joining the turnpike road — once to deliver the notes to the Grange and once outside Robert's lodgings, to allow him to toss a few necessaries into his knapsack.

Every minute of waiting was agony to Ellen. If Maggie had not been with her, she might have urged the coachman to set out without Robert. And yet, apart from Maggie, she could think of nobody she would rather have had with her.

It was almost completely dark by the time they were finally on their way, but the coachman had instructions to travel through the night, hiring post horses along the way — a situation that alarmed Ellen. Surely the only reason for so much haste and expense was that Jemmy's condition was critical?

'What if he's dead before we arrive?' she whispered. Hitherto she had thought the worst that could happen was to be denied custody of Jemmy. But this was far worse.

Maggie put her arm around her waist and Robert leaned forward to clasp her hand. She knew they wanted to reassure her, but dared not because they knew how implacable Mr Fairfax was. He would not take alarm or pander to anything he would see as his grandson's whims unless there was a serious cause for concern.

The very thought that she had been taking part in the frivolities at her cousin's wedding while her son was ill and needed her made Ellen feel sick.

'What exactly did Mr Fairfax say in his letter?' Robert asked.

Ellen shook her head.

'It was Mrs Fairfax who wrote,' she said. 'She — she — ' She groped to remember the exact wording her mother-in-law had used since it was far too dark by now to make out the letter. 'She says Jemmy has a high fever and he won't stop crying. That's all I can remember. Oh God, what shall I do if he dies?'

'Don't even think about that yet,' Robert murmured, as Maggie rocked Ellen against herself as if she was a child needing to be soothed.

'Maybe it's a false alarm. Maybe Jemmy is better already,' Robert went on, but Ellen shook her head against Maggie's shoulder.

'And what if he isn't?'

'Ellen, you can't — you mustn't anticipate the worst,' he urged. 'Not yet. If it happens, then we'll deal with it somehow. But for the moment, we must cling to what hope there is for as long as we can.' He added softly, 'I — we'll take care of you.'

And even in the midst of her desolation, Ellen felt a tiny flame warm her soul.

* * *

Dawn was staining the horizon pink and tangerine and primrose by the time the coach pulled up outside Ashton Hall. But Ellen felt far too numb to appreciate the beauty of the morning.

She had woken, stiff and dazed, at the clang of the main gates. It seemed to her the driveway had never been so long before, nor the house so vast and cold, the white stucco gleaming ghost-like in the still-weak light. She peered upwards as she clambered out of the coach, looking for some clue, even though she knew the windows of the night nursery were not visible from the front of the house.

But it was too early in the morning. Curtains and shutters might have been closed as a sign of mourning — or simply because the household was barely stirring yet. Even so, her heart leapt in terror. It must have been at least twelve hours since Mrs Fairfax had written that letter. Anything might have happened in the interval.

'Courage, Ellen,' Robert murmured as he gripped her hand.

There was no time for her to reply.

The sound of a key in a lock cut through the still morning air, as if the earliness of the hour had somehow magnified the sound. Moving stiffly after the long, cramped journey and almost sleepless night, Ellen tottered towards the flight of steps that led to the main entrance. Maggie's petticoats rustled against hers. Robert's arm brushed her sleeve.

The servant who had drawn the bolts on the door stood aside and Ellen steeled herself for an encounter with Mr Fairfax. Instead, an ineffectual wisp of a woman wafted out of the vast entrance hall.

'Oh dear, oh dear, I didn't know what to do for the best, really I didn't,' Mrs Fairfax said, her thin, fluttering voice rolling all the words indiscriminately into a single sentence. She seemed barely conscious that Ellen had not come alone. Her daughter-in-law grasped her by both hands.

'How is he? Is he still alive?'

Mrs Fairfax seemed startled by

Ellen's vehemence, as if she had been woken too suddenly from a dream.

'Yes, yes, he's still alive, at least he was when I last asked, oh dear, I am glad you are here — I think.' The last two words wavered.

This was the nearest Mrs Fairfax had ever come to expressing an opinion of her own, as far as Ellen was aware.

'In that case, I should like to see my son,' Ellen said as forcefully as she dared because she hoped Mrs Fairfax would not remember any prohibitions against her.

'Oh, yes, yes, of course. I did do the right thing, didn't I, in sending for you?'

Ellen felt something icy slide down her spine, like a drop from an overhanging bough of a tree. There was something she had not been told; she knew it instinctively.

'Of course you did,' she replied nonetheless, leading the way boldly into the house as Mrs Fairfax scurried alongside her. 'You remember Maggie, don't you? And Mr Lester is the brother-in-law of my cousin Philip Longridge and a family friend.'

'Charmed — delighted — ' Mrs Fairfax muttered distractedly, barely glancing at Ellen's companions. 'It's just that everything is at sixes and sevens and — oh dear . . . '

'I take it Jemmy is in the old nursery?' Ellen cut ruthlessly across Mrs Fairfax's mumbling, realising that was the only way to obtain the information she wanted.

'Yes, but — '

'Excuse me,' Ellen interrupted her again with the most charming smile she could muster in the circumstances. 'I'm sure you will make my companions welcome, but I really cannot wait a second longer.'

The words were barely out of her mouth before Ellen was flying up the wide staircase, clutching two handfuls of petticoats to keep them out of the way. She felt her gown flare out behind her like a comet's tail.

In the dark watches of the night, she had been terrified that she had forgotten the geography of this house. But as she ran, she knew instinctively which corridor to take, what she would see around the next corner, where the stairs to the attic floor were hidden. On the top floor, she startled a maid, who flinched against the wall like a petrified rabbit as Ellen dashed past.

She was gasping for breath by the time she reached the nursery door. She paused a moment in the corridor, trying desperately to still her panting and catch any sound from the nursery. But the room was deathly silent.

Ellen shuddered at the adjective. Then she steeled herself. She had to know. She had to remain strong, whatever the outcome. She had to see her son.

She didn't knock, not wanting to disturb Jemmy if he was asleep, even though more than anything she wanted him to fling his arms around her neck, cling to her like a monkey, beg her never to leave him again.

She barely noticed the nursemaid, whose head twisted round at the sound of her footsteps. Ellen saw only the little truckle bed, the mop of fair, fever-tangled hair above the sheet.

As she came closer, she got a better view of his face, the whorl of his ear, the little, half-clenched fist on which his cheek rested. Ellen's heart rolled over with love, only to be seized by a sudden rush of fear.

The blankets weren't moving. She couldn't see him breathing. His cheeks looked flushed, but perhaps that was only the effect of the early morning light. With a low, inarticulate cry, she dropped on her knees beside the truckle bed. Her fingers stretched out tenta-tively for Jemmy's cheek, needing to know if he was alive, but unwilling to wake him if he was asleep.

'Madam,' the nursemaid whispered urgently.

Jemmy's skin was burning. His lips fluttered and he uttered a little sigh, as if he had recognised her touch and knew that all was well now. Something wooden protruded from beneath his pillow and when Ellen extracted it, she discovered it was the little horse Robert had given her son. She couldn't help wondering whether Jemmy or his nursemaid had put it there, as a reminder of his past life.

'The doctor was here about an hour ago,' the nursemaid whispered. 'He said if the fever broke soon, he'd pull through.'

Ellen's vision blurred as she glanced up at the sensible-looking girl who had been with Mr Fairfax and his lawyer on that terrible day.

'Thank you for taking care of my son,' she said.

* * *

After that, time ceased to have any meaning. Minutes might have passed, or hours. The fire whispered on the hearth. Jemmy snuffled in his sleep.

Muted voices — Robert's, Maggie's, Mrs Fairfax's — came and went.

It gave Ellen a shock when she glanced up and found Maggie beside her. If she had thought about it at all, she might have guessed that the nursemaid had been sent to rest after her long vigil. But such matters seemed hopelessly trivial to her now.

Despite her best intentions, she knew she must have drowsed, kneeling on the floor, with her head beside Jemmy's on the pillow because she wanted her face to be the first thing he saw when he woke. There had been vague attempts to persuade her to go and rest too, but she had resisted them all. She had an unreasoning conviction that if she left her son's bedside for even a second, she would never be allowed back.

She was roused by a tap at the door. She lifted her head and met Maggie's eye.

'I'll go,' the maid said, heaving herself to her feet.

Ellen didn't argue. She turned her gaze back towards her son. But the sound of Robert's voice, asking for her, caught her attention. She must have been soundly asleep not to have heard his crutches and wooden leg on the uncarpeted floorboards of the attic.

There was an ache across her chest where she had been leaning against the wooden frame of the bed, but she hauled herself upright. Jemmy's lashes barely fluttered as Ellen tiptoed across the creaking floorboards to the door.

'What is it?' she asked.

Robert hesitated and glanced over her shoulder towards the little bed. Something about his anxious expression caused Ellen to slip out of the nursery into the corridor and close the door behind her.

'What is it?' she repeated.

Robert shifted his weight uncomfortably.

'I've had a long conversation with Mrs Fairfax,' he said. 'It seems her husband is away from home, but is expected hourly to return in reply to her summons. He has no idea his wife sent for you in a moment of desperation and uncertainty when she thought Jemmy might die.' He hesitated to utter the last word, but Ellen shuddered nonetheless.

'Thank you for the warning.'

Her heart sank at the prospect of an interview with her former father-in-law. At the best of times he was not a man to listen to explanations and if he worked himself into a rage, his wife would be far too timid to interrupt him. Ellen knew that simply by being here she was probably in breach of the law.

As if in answer to her fears, she caught the sound of hooves and the rattle of a coach outside.

'Heavens, do you think that might be him?' she asked, raising stricken eyes to Robert's face. There were no windows in this passage from which they could have seen the front of the house. 'Whatever shall we do?'

Robert seemed to make a hasty decision.

'Go back to Jemmy,' he said. 'I'll go and talk to him — if he will listen.'

16

Robert had no more wish to confront Mr Fairfax than Ellen did, but he felt it was his duty. After all, he had done precious little since their arrival, apart from sitting with Mrs Fairfax, listening to her endless twittering and trying to reassure her that she had done the right thing. He had even let her show him a portrait of her son and listened to her tales about what a fine man James had been.

He hoped that while Ellen was in the nursery, she would be safe. Surely not even Mr Fairfax would want to disturb Jemmy while he was so ill? Even so, Robert limped as rapidly as he could through the labyrinth of the attic floor, thanking God for his good sense of direction. But he dared not rush the first flight of stairs. He would be no use whatsoever if he fell and injured himself.

By the time he reached the top of the main staircase, Mr Fairfax had evidently disembarked from his coach. Robert could hear his voice below, asking after *the boy*.

'Oh dear, oh dear, I'm sure I don't know, that is, I asked of course and I have been to see him, but . . . '

'Is he better or worse?'

'Yes. I mean, no. I mean — oh dear, I'm so confused.'

Mr Fairfax uttered an impatient snort, like a beleaguered bull. Robert heard his footsteps drumming on the stairs.

'Oh, but I should warn you . . . ' Mrs Fairfax faltered, her voice fainter than ever.

As Mr Fairfax rounded the curve of the staircase, Robert uttered a low cough to attract his attention. The older man's head shot up.

'Who the devil are you, sir?'

Robert saw from the older man's frown that he recognised him, but could not place where he had seen him.

Recalling Ellen's introduction, he announced, 'My name is Lieutenant Robert Lester, late of the 45th Regiment. I'm the brother-in-law of Mr Philip Longridge.'

Mr Fairfax's expression did not relax one jot. He grunted.

'Perhaps I should have asked what the devil you are doing in my house,' he replied with heavy sarcasm, coming another step further up to reduce the difference in height between them.

Mrs Fairfax too had scuttled partway up the stairs, but now she pulled her head into her shoulders, like a snail into its shell, waiting for the storm to break.

'I accompanied Mrs James Fairfax here from Nottinghamshire.' Robert kept his voice soft to hide his agitation.

He was not sure whether he should add that Ellen had been sent for, thus incriminating the elder Mrs Fairfax, or let Mr Fairfax assume that their arrival while Jemmy was ill was purely coincidental.

The decision was taken out of his hands.

'I didn't know what else to do,' Mrs Fairfax fluttered. 'You were away and the poor child was so very ill and wouldn't stop crying for his mother and the doctor said the distress would kill him if I didn't — didn't — '

Like a clockwork toy whose key had wound down, she stuttered to a halt under her husband's glare.

Robert braced himself for an explosion.

'You invited *that woman* into this house?'

'The — the doctor said . . . '

Mr Fairfax emitted another snort, as if his wife were a persistent fly buzzing around his head. His mouth hardened and, with an agility Robert had not expected from a man of his age, he began to lope up the staircase.

'I beg you, sir, don't do anything rash. Your grandson is in a very delicate state,' Robert urged, trying to bar his way.

But Mr Fairfax barged straight past, knocking Robert off-balance. He staggered back and might have fallen, had he not crashed against the wainscoting.

It was a nightmare. He couldn't allow Mr Fairfax to bear down on Ellen in his current mood. Righting himself with a supreme effort, Robert propelled himself after the older man, trying to close the gap that was opening up between them. And there was still one more staircase to negotiate. Robert knew that if he let Mr Fairfax mount those stairs, he would never catch up.

'What would your son think?' Robert thought he saw Mr Fairfax waver and he pressed his advantage. 'Ellen is the woman he loved. Without her, he might have died heirless.'

The gambit worked.

'You're a damned impertinent pup.' Mr Fairfax whisked round to glare at Robert from the foot of the attic stairs.

'But you know I'm right.' Robert met the other man's stare fearlessly.

'You know nothing about my son, or

how that woman entrapped him. She isn't fit to bring up a child. She's morally and financially bankrupt.'

'If you were twenty years younger, I would call you out for such a slander.'

A whimper behind him betrayed the presence of Mrs Fairfax, but Robert was too furious to back down.

'The rumours about Ellen's reputation only arose because of her kindness to a stranger in need. And I am more than willing to repair the damage I have done her by marrying her.'

An ugly sneer distorted Mr Fairfax's face.

'Oh, so it's *Ellen* now, is it? I suppose you think that by marrying that woman, you'll get your hands on my fortune. Let me tell you, if she does marry you, I'll disown her son as well as her.'

For a long moment, Robert stared at the other man, struggling to get his temper under control.

'You really know nothing about human nature,' he said. 'I'd marry Ellen if she were a beggar on the streets. I'd care for Jemmy as if he were my own and encourage Ellen to tell him what a good man his real father was as soon as he is old enough to understand. I'd far, far rather toil for every penny, every crust of bread to feed them than to accept any man's charity. There is *nothing* I wouldn't do for them.'

In the echoing silence that followed, Robert's attention was drawn by the tiniest whisper of a sound above. The scuff of a foot, perhaps. Dazed, he raised his head.

Ellen was standing at the top of the narrow staircase. Robert's heart jolted. That look on her face — could it mean that Jemmy was worse? Or — or — but he dared not complete that thought.

Her cheeks reddened and she swallowed visibly as her father-in-law, following Robert's gaze, turned likewise towards her.

At the sight of her, Mr Fairfax uttered an inarticulate cry of rage and began to hurtle up the stairs. Ellen shrank back, but Robert, urged on by some impulse, propelled himself towards the foot of the stairs.

'Wait!'

He was too late. In his haste, Mr Fairfax missed his footing. He fell, as if some invisible force had tugged him by the ankle. There was a sickening thud as he struck the wooden treads, followed by further clatters as he juddered down the stairs, his arms stretched above his head, in a final attempt to seize his prey, or to save himself.

Robert threw himself down on the stairs to block the inexorable descent of the older man and behind him, he heard Mrs Fairfax's thin wail of despair.

★   ★   ★

For what seemed like hours, Ellen was frozen. She roused herself at the sight of Robert crouched beside her father-in-law, trying to ascertain the extent of his injuries. She pattered down the stairs as quickly as she could, slipping in her hurry but catching the handrail just in time.

'He's unconscious, but he's still breathing,' Robert said. 'We need to call a doctor.'

Fortunately, alerted by the crash, some of the servants had already begun to appear. Mr Fairfax's fall had left Ellen shaken and nauseous, but she felt it was her duty to stay, though her heart yearned to be with Jemmy.

'How is Jemmy? He isn't worse, is he?'

Robert's words cut through her trance-like state.

'No, there's no change,' she said. 'Maggie is still with him, but I couldn't let you fight my battles alone.'

Robert clasped her hand and warmth flooded through her.

'Go back to the nursery,' he said. 'Leave everything else to me.'

'Are you sure?' Ellen glanced at her father-in-law. His mouth had dropped open as his breath rasped in his chest.

'I'm sure. Jemmy needs you. I'll send

you word of Mr Fairfax's condition as soon as we know anything.'

Ellen stumbled to her feet. The stairs had never seemed so steep or so numerous before. At the top, she glanced back. The menservants had gathered around their master to carry him to his room.

There's nothing I can do for him. He wouldn't even want me at his bedside, Ellen told herself. But a nasty little whisper taunted her.

This is all my fault. If he hadn't been so infuriated by my presence. If I hadn't been at the top of the stairs. If . . .

But Robert was right. Her anxiety about Jemmy was stronger than every other emotion. What if there had been some change while she had been away? It felt as if hours must have passed, though with her conscious mind, she knew it could have only have been a matter of minutes. The floorboards seemed to undulate beneath her feet, like a rowing boat on a calm day, but she forced herself on.

Maggie's head whisked round at the sound of the door.

'No change,' she whispered, 'but sleep is the best medicine. It will all come right in the — there's something else, isn't there?'

Her whisper grew fierce, as she caught sight of Ellen's expression.

'What has that man said to you?' she demanded and Ellen almost expected her to roll up her sleeves, as if she intended to take on Mr Fairfax in a bare-knuckle fight. 'I knew it was a bad idea to let you go.'

Ellen shook her head.

'He — he's had a fall,' she croaked. 'He's badly hurt and it's all my fault.'

Her voice quavered. *Why am I crying for a man who hates me, when I haven't cried for my own son?* But every time Ellen closed her eyes, she could see Mr Fairfax thudding down the stairs again, the anger in his face turning to panic.

Maggie's arms were suddenly around

her. She rocked Ellen and murmured reassurances, as if she were no older than Jemmy. And as the tension eased in Ellen's chest, she felt another warming sensation creep over her at the memory of Robert's passionate declaration that there was nothing he would not do for her and Jemmy.

★ ★ ★

Time seemed to crawl until Ellen finally heard the cautious tapping of Robert's crutches. She rose stiffly to greet him. His eyes were grave as they met hers.

'The doctor is with Mr Fairfax,' he said. 'He'll be here presently.'

'How is he?' Ellen asked. 'Mr Fairfax, I mean.'

Robert shook his head.

'He seems to be having trouble breathing,' he said. 'The doctor thinks he might have broken a rib and it might have pierced his lungs.'

Ellen shuddered. Without warning, Robert lurched towards her.

'It was an accident, Ellen. Nobody is to blame, least of all you,' he said and Ellen shivered again, this time at his apparent ability to read her mind.

'I wish I could believe you,' she replied.

But a sound from the truckle bed cut the conversation short. Ellen was instantly on her knees. Jemmy's eyelids were open a slit and she could see his eyeballs dancing in the grip of a nightmare. His fever-cracked lips were parted to emit tiny whimpers that tore at her heart.

'Don't cry, Jemmy. Mamma's here. Everything will be better soon. Don't cry, darling.'

She stroked his tangled hair away from his over-hot forehead as Robert eased himself down on the floor beside her.

'What's all this then, little man?' Robert murmured. 'We can't let a mere illness defeat you, can we?'

But Ellen could hear the fear behind his attempted cheerfulness.

With a sob, Jemmy opened his eyes.

'Mamma?' he croaked.

'Yes, Jemmy, I'm here. I'm here at last.'

She saw tears swimming in her son's eyes and she had to blink to prevent herself from crying too.

'Mamma,' he whispered again, raising his arms.

Ellen gathered him to her, blankets and all, so she could kiss his hot forehead. The weight, the warmth of his body against her made her feel complete for the first time since she had lost him.

'Look who else has come to see you,' she said, turning him towards Robert.

A faint smile wavered on Jemmy's lips.

'Misty Lesty,' he murmured before he began to cough.

A shadow fall across Ellen. She looked up to take a glass of water from Maggie.

'Maggie's here too,' Ellen said, holding the glass to Jemmy's lips. 'We

314

all came because Grandmamma wrote to say you were ill.'

'Go home now?' Jemmy murmured sleepily. He pushed the glass away and snuggled back against her breast.

A spasm of pain darted through Ellen, but she kissed him again and replied, 'You're not well enough to go anywhere, young man. Now close your eyes and go to sleep like a good boy and — and we'll talk more when you're better.'

Jemmy did not argue. That in itself showed how weak he must be. His eyes were shut before his head touched his pillow, but he took the precaution of grasping the ruffle of his mother's sleeve, to try to ensure that Ellen could not slip away without him noticing.

Ellen couldn't take her eyes from him. Jemmy's innocent question had opened up the chasm of uncertainty she had been trying to ignore. She had no idea what would happen to Jemmy, whether Mr Fairfax lived or died.

She turned her head at the sound of

the door. It was not until the family doctor came forward to examine Jemmy that Ellen realised Mrs Fairfax had been hiding in his shadow, smaller, more lost than ever, her eyes wide as if she would never close them again.

'How is Mr Fairfax?' Ellen asked, suddenly gripped by a premonition.

The doctor's look unnerved her and even before he spoke, she knew. Perhaps Robert guessed too. He clasped Ellen's hand.

'There was nothing I could do,' the doctor said. 'Mr Fairfax died a few minutes ago.'

17

Ellen raised her face to the sun. The golden light seemed only to heighten the scarlets and yellows of the regimented rows of tulips in the symmetrical flowerbeds. Not a blade of grass was permitted to peep through the gravel of the paths. Not a single cushion of moss had insinuated itself into the crevices of the sundial's plinth.

She needed fresh air. Her head felt thick with the muzziness of the sickroom. She had even lost track of how long she had been at Ashton Hall.

She was clad in black once more. *So much for Caroline's attempts to get me back into colours*, Ellen thought wistfully.

'Mamma!'

Jemmy's voice roused her. She turned to see him charging towards her. It was the first time the doctor had permitted him to set foot outdoors. Even then he had been adamant that it could not be for more than half an hour. The spring air still had a nip.

Ellen crouched and allowed Jemmy to crash straight into her outstretched arms, so she could gather him up. He seemed to tire more easily than before his illness. Evidently it would take time for him to regain his strength.

'We'll have to take him inside soon,' Maggie said.

She had been in close attendance, following Jemmy wherever his adventurous little legs would carry him.

'I know,' Ellen replied, turning to look at the house.

She still could not love it. In her mind, it was associated too much with her first months of widowhood. She could not seem to persuade herself that this house must, surely, now belong to Jemmy and not the man she had feared for so long.

She knew Mr Fairfax's will had to be read, but she dreaded the prospect.

She had almost enjoyed the hiatus, while arrangements were made for the inquest and funeral. Jemmy had recovered slowly, first sitting up in bed, then being allowed to sit on the drawing room sofa, because Mrs Fairfax found consolation in feeding him delicacies, listening to his prattle and dredging up stories from long ago to tell him in her usual wavering manner.

But Ellen knew this was only a temporary reprieve. Mr Fairfax was bound to have made provisions in his will to take care of Jemmy and Ashton Hall and, quite possibly, separate her from her son once more.

It was Robert who had dealt with all the practicalities, giving evidence at Mr Fairfax's inquest and arranging the funeral, while Ellen had still been too preoccupied in the nursery and Mrs Fairfax had been too dazed to do anything at all.

The crunch of gravel made Ellen turn. As if her thoughts had conjured him up, Robert was standing at the top of a short flight of steps leading down to the formal garden from the terrace. He smiled, but his eyes remained grave.

'It's time,' he said.

★ ★ ★

A long silence settled on the elegant drawing room after Mr Green had stopped speaking. Mrs Fairfax looked smaller than ever, huddled on the sofa, her eyes like those of a frightened rabbit.

Ellen could hardly believe what she had heard. Unable to sit still a moment longer, she walked to the window, to stare sightlessly at the formal garden in which, just half an hour ago, she and Maggie had been with Jemmy. Of all the possible outcomes of the reading of the will, this was the only one she had never envisaged.

Mr Green had hummed and ha-ed for some minutes before coming to the point.

'Mr Fairfax was in the process of having a new will drawn up, but he died before he could sign it.'

'He died intestate?' Ellen asked.

'No, no, there is an earlier will, but it was drawn up shortly after the death of Captain Fairfax.'

He had gone on to list all the provisions of that will — chiefly that Jemmy would inherit Ashton Hall when he was twenty-one, but that Mrs Fairfax was to be permitted to live there for the remainder of her life.

'What about my son's minority?' Ellen's voice was so hoarse, she was surprised anyone could make out her words. 'Who has custody of him?'

'Ah.' Mr Green cleared his throat and looked down at his papers. 'Under the terms of the magistrate's writ, custody was to be shared by Mr and Mrs Fairfax until the case could be brought to court. It was only ever intended as a temporary measure, but as things stand, Mrs Fairfax is the boy's legal guardian.'

'Me?' Mrs Fairfax squeaked.

Ellen's heart beat hard, afraid of letting her hopes rise too soon, for fear that something would thwart them.

'You would be quite within your rights, madam, to follow your late husband's wishes and apply for permanent custody ... ' Mr Green was continuing, but Mrs Fairfax squeaked again.

'Oh dear, go to court, you mean, and take the poor child away from his mother? Heavens, no, I could never, it would be much too distressing, no, no, far better for his mother to have him back ... '

Mr Green began a rambling speech, to reassure her that she should not have to lift a finger, except to pay her legal representative to act on her behalf, but Robert, who had been silent hitherto, intervened.

'Perhaps Mrs Fairfax needs more time to decide,' he suggested.

'Oh no, no, I don't need time at all, my mind is quite made up,' Mrs Fairfax broke in, then stopped and reddened, apparently embarrassed by this uncharacteristic display of decisiveness.

'I'm sure we shouldn't keep you any longer, sir, you must be very busy,' she added in her usual, more timid tones.

She rose and as Robert too hauled himself to his feet, Mr Green was obliged to do the same, acknowledging himself to have been dismissed.

The instant the door had closed behind him, Ellen darted across the room to embrace her startled mother-in-law.

'I cannot thank you enough,' she whispered.

'Oh, my dear, it's nothing, it's only what's right, there has been so much unhappiness in this family already. But you will stay, won't you? I couldn't bear it, being in this big house alone, I wouldn't know what to do with myself, or how to run the place, Mr Fairfax did *everything*. So impatient with me. I've never been much good at that sort of thing. I wasn't brought up to be a great lady, you see,' she trailed off apologetically.

Ellen felt torn. She wanted nothing more than to escape from Ashton Hall. It was on the tip of her tongue to say *she* had not been born to such grandeur either. But there was something so forlorn about Mrs Fairfax.

'I — I don't know. I need time to think.'

Even at these gentle words, Mrs Fairfax seemed to wilt.

Ellen thought wistfully of the steward's cottage in which she had been so happy. Ashton Hall had always seemed too large to make a comfortable home.

But perhaps I could change that, she thought. After all, she owed Mrs Fairfax something for giving up her claim to Jemmy.

'Perhaps we could stay,' Ellen began slowly and then caught sight of Robert's expression, just before he turned away.

'Excuse me,' he murmured, as Mrs Fairfax began to pour out her gratitude.

* ★ * ★ * ★

Ellen found him in an isolated part of the garden, sitting on a bench she knew only too well. She crept up behind him and sat down next to him.

'I used to come here a lot,' she said, 'when I needed to be alone with my memories of James or escape the restrictions of the house.' She gestured towards the glimpse of countryside visible from this slope, beyond the high, stone wall. 'I used to think if I could get beyond that wall, I would be free and — content, if not happy.'

She sensed Robert flickering a glance towards her as she spoke.

'And yet you are choosing to make Ashton Hall your home,' he said in neutral tones.

Ellen turned towards him, but he continued staring at the view.

'No, I'm not *choosing* this. I have no choice. You've seen how helpless Mrs Fairfax is. And she has done a wonderful thing, giving Jemmy back to me. I can't desert her, now she needs me.'

'No, of course not,' he said, finally turning towards her. He mustered a wry smile. 'But I shall miss you — and Jemmy and Maggie too.'

It was what Ellen had feared. She had wanted to follow Robert as soon as he left the drawing room, but Mrs Fairfax had needed her attention, until Ellen had finally persuaded her that a nap might do her good.

'You're going back to Nottingham-shire?' Ellen asked.

'My family is there and my work.'

'Yes, of course.'

Ellen dropped her head. She had allowed herself to hope. That was the trouble. She had turned the words of Robert's declaration of love over and over in her mind, during the dark watches of the night, while she had sat by Jemmy's sickbed.

She hadn't been able to predict what provisions Mr Fairfax had made for Jemmy, but she had hoped that, no matter how hard the fight for her son might be, Robert would be by her side. It had never occurred to her that she might regain her son, but lose the man she loved.

'I had hoped you might stay,' she said, but her voice was unsteady.

'How can I? I need to earn a living, for my own self-respect, if for no other reason.'

'You wouldn't consider staying on as — as Mrs Fairfax's steward?'

Robert flickered another glance at her. Then, as if making a sudden decision, he pressed his lips together and hauled himself to his feet.

'Please, don't tempt me.'

'Would it be so bad if you succumbed?' Ellen urged. 'None of us wants to lose you. Mrs Fairfax says she doesn't know what she would have done without you since her husband's death and Jemmy loves you like a favourite uncle — or a father.'

She could see in profile the downward sweep of Robert's lashes.

'Even Maggie says she is fond of you.'

'And you?' Robert's voice cracked. 'What do *you* feel about me?'

'I — ' Ellen felt heat flood into her cheeks, knowing that her next words could change the whole course of her life. Gathering her courage, she raised her chin. 'I love you, Robert. I'm not ashamed to admit it. If there is anything I learnt from being married to a soldier, it is that life and love are precious and shouldn't be squandered.'

'Ellen.'

The suppressed emotion in his voice made a surge of hope rush into her breast. Then he turned away.

'No, it's impossible,' he said. 'I don't belong here. I'm just a servant's son . . . '

'And when have I ever cared about such things?' Ellen swept past him to block his way. 'You said you would marry me if I were a beggar on the streets. Why can you not love me now that my son is rich? Or did you not

328

mean what you said — that there was nothing you wouldn't do for me and Jemmy?'

Her voice broke and she was forced to drop her head to hide her tears.

'Yes, I meant every word.' Robert tucked his crutch more firmly under his arm so he could free one hand to grasp her sleeve. 'Don't you think I would propose to you, if I had anything to offer you?'

She could see by his expression how torn he was.

'You could offer me yourself,' she said. 'I am not rich. I still only have the money James left me in his will. We could live modestly. We could do anything we wanted. Or is public opinion and masculine pride more important to you?'

'Can't you see that pride is all I have left?'

Ellen felt her whole body slump.

'If that's how you feel, perhaps you are right,' she said. 'If Jemmy and I mean so little to you, perhaps it is better that you go.'

She wrenched herself free and began to stride away, though she could barely see where she was going.

'Ellen!'

It was the despairing tone in his cry that made her stop. She heard his approach.

'Ellen, I'm sorry. I — ' One of his crutches clattered to the ground as he pulled her to his breast. 'Ellen, don't. Please don't cry. I can't bear it.'

She felt the warmth of his body as he drew her closer. He was shaking and she realised that with only one crutch, he was dependent on her to help him keep his balance.

'I'm sorry,' he murmured. 'You're right. I know you're right. God knows I don't want to hurt you, when I love you so much. It's just — it's hard, being dependent on the goodwill of others . . .'

'Oh, don't worry. We'll make you earn your keep if you do stay.' From somewhere Ellen mustered a smile.

She wasn't expecting him to swoop down and kiss her, but she yielded willingly.

'We'll work something out,' she murmured, as they clung to one another. 'You'll see. It will all come right somehow.'

We do hope that you have enjoyed reading this large print book.

Did you know that all of our titles are available for purchase?

We publish a wide range of high quality large print books including:
Romances, Mysteries, Classics
General Fiction
Non Fiction and Westerns

Special interest titles available in large print are:
The Little Oxford Dictionary
Music Book, Song Book
Hymn Book, Service Book

Also available from us courtesy of Oxford University Press:
Young Readers' Dictionary
(large print edition)
Young Readers' Thesaurus
(large print edition)

For further information or a free brochure, please contact us at:
Ulverscroft Large Print Books Ltd.,
The Green, Bradgate Road, Anstey,
Leicester, LE7 7FU, England.
Tel: (00 44) 0116 236 4325
Fax: (00 44) 0116 234 0205

A TEMPORARY AFFAIR

Carol MacLean

Cass Bryson is persuaded by her twin sister Lila to attend a celebrity party in her stead, accompanying the enigmatic photographer Finn Mallory. Then, when his secretary falls ill, he asks Cass to take over her job temporarily. Though she can't deny her attraction to her new boss, Cass is lacking in self-confidence, not least because of the scars she bears from a tragic accident. But Finn is drawn to Cass too, and it seems they might just find love together — until Lila returns, determined to capture his heart for herself . . .

THE RUBY

Fay Cunningham

Cass finds her friend Michael dead in his swimming pool, and while drowning appears at first to be the cause, evidence mounts that foul play was involved. The investigation brings the handsome Detective Inspector Noel Raven into Cass's life — and the connection between the two is literally electrifying. Cass's mother, a witch, warns her that she may be in deadly danger; only by working together can Cass and Noel hope to overcome the evil forces at work. Though Cass finds that her gemstones are also handy in a pinch . . .

FRANCESCA

Susan Udy

When her sister Francesca disappears, Jamie is determined to unravel the truth. Keeping her identity a secret, she inveigles her way into the household where Francesca lived with her husband, the compelling Alexander Whittaker: wildlife expert, broadcaster — and Francesca's possible murderer. He was seen arguing with her just hours before she vanished, and evidence mounts up that he knew she'd been having an affair. Playing detective becomes a dangerous game for Jamie, especially when she realises she has lost her heart to the prime suspect . . .

BENEATH AN OUTBACK SKY

Noelene Jenkinson

Sophie Nash's outback pastoral station in South Australia's panoramic Flinders Ranges is in danger of going under, unless she can find another source of revenue. So when charismatic geologist Charlie Kendall arrives to camp on her property with his students, love is the last thing on her mind. In fact, Sophie has seen personal loss devastate her family and has vowed never to lose her heart. But Charlie's charms are hard to resist, and his family might just have the solution to her problems . . .

MARIAH'S MARRIAGE

Anne Stenhouse

1822: Scholarly Mariah Fox is fiercely dedicated to her work of educating London urchins. When she is charged by a stray pig, and quite literally falls into the arms of Tobias Longreach, her life changes forever . . . For Tobias, the Earl of Mellon, requires a wife to provide an heir — and decides that Mariah will do very nicely. But the sinister Sir Lucas Wellwood, burdened by debt, has been urging his sister Araminta to secure Tobias's hand for herself — and will stop at nothing to get his hands on the earl's wealth . . .

REGAN'S FALL

Valerie Holmes

After the death of their father and the removal of their gentle mother to debtors' prison, Regan and her brother Isaac are left in desperate circumstances. Their only hope is to appeal for aid from an estranged relative at Marram Hall, Lady Arianne, whom neither sibling has ever met. Upon her arrival, Regan encounters the handsome and masterful James Coldwell, the local magistrate, but fears that if she trusts him he will throw her and Isaac out of the house — or worse. Then Lady Arianne attempts to do just that . . .